Anne G. Faigen

NEW WORLD WAITING

by

ANNE G. FAIGEN

The Local History Company
publishers of history and heritage

Pittsburgh, Pennsylvania, USA

New World Waiting
Copyright © 2006 by Anne G. Faigen

Published by
The Local History Company
112 North Woodland Road
Pittsburgh, PA 15232
www.TheLocalHistoryCompany.com   info@TheLocalHistoryCompany.com

The name "The Local History Company", "Publishers of History and Heritage", and its logo are trademarks of The Local History Company.

Image of girl's dress on the cover derived from a photo in the collection of Roger Vaughan (http://www.cartes.freeuk.com/index.htm). Courtesy of Roger Vaughan.
Image of girl's face on the cover derived from a photo in the collection of Christine Cooper. Courtesy of Christine Cooper.
Panorama of 1905 Pittsburgh derived from a photo in the collection of the Library of Congress, LOC Prints and Photographs Division, LC-USZ62-110668.

ISBN-13: 978-0-9744715-5-6
ISBN-10: 0-9744715-5-0

Library of Congress Cataloging-in-Publication Data

Faigen, Anne G.
   New World Waiting / by Anne G. Faigen.
           p.   cm.
   Summary: While living with her mother in 1900 Pittsburgh and waiting for her father and brother to arrive from Poland, fifteen-year-old Molly adapts to American life with some help from her schoolteacher, Willa Cather.
   ISBN-13: 978-0-9744715-5-6 (softcover : alk. paper)
   ISBN-10: 0-9744715-5-0 (softcover)
   [1. Immigrants—Fiction. 2. Polish Americans—Fiction. 3. Jews—United States—Fiction. 4. Cather, Willa, 1873-1947—Fiction. 5. Social settlements—Fiction. 6. Pittsburgh (Pa.)—History—20th century—Fiction.] I. Title.
PZ7.F1433New 2005
[Fic]—dc22
                              2005026370
Printed in the United States

DEDICATION

For Arielle, Russell, and Eric—may your
own new worlds be joyful and fulfilling.

AUTHOR'S NOTE

Although some of the events in this novel are based on local history—Willa Cather's first professional employment after her graduation from the University of Nebraska was, indeed, at a publication office in Pittsburgh, and she did teach Latin, then English in two city high schools—the other characters and events in *New World Waiting* are fictional. Willa Cather's dialogue is invented, except for her actual writing, which is italicized or otherwise indicated.

I would like to thank Christine Cooper for her thoughtful and sensitive work as editor; George Shames for promoting the novel's publication; and Mark Faigen for his encouragement, support, and technical assistance.

ONE

Pushing a broom across the grimy wooden floor, Molly stopped to brush away the feathers that tickled her nose and threatened a siege of sneezing. Finally finished, she piled the sweepings, heavy with black grit from mill smoke and dotted with the feathers of slaughtered chickens, into a newspaper funnel and carried it outside to dump at the curb. Outdoors, the sour air reeked of mill smoke. Specks of soot swirled like snowflakes in thin rays of sunlight.

Molly's glance up and down the crowded sidewalk revealed no sign of Uncle Abe. With a sigh and shake of her head, she re-entered her uncle's poultry store, knowing she would be late. She pulled a handkerchief from her pocket and wiped it across her damp forehead, frowning at the dark smudges on the white cloth. There was no way to keep clean in this place, she thought.

Molly and Cleo had been planning the streetcar ride to Schenley Park all week. They'd saved their pennies and talked their friend Vittorio—or Victor as he insisted on being called—into meeting them near the fountain with the towering statue in the middle. It was hot, even for July, but they'd wade in the fountain's pool, walk through the grass barefooted, and eat their lunch under the canopy of leaves that provided a cool escape from Pittsburgh's heat and smoke.

Because Molly's mother had a fever and needed to rest this morning, Molly had taken her place at the store. Uncle Abe was off doing errands; she could leave when he returned, but he'd been gone for hours and there was still no sign of him.

Wasn't that just like Uncle Abe, Molly thought, slamming the broom into a closet at the back of the store. Sometimes he treated them, especially Mama, as if they were servants, not relatives. When she complained Mama told her she mustn't be ungrateful. If not for Abe they'd still be in Swidnik, the town in Poland where she'd been born.

When she and Mama arrived three years ago, in 1897, she was nearly twelve, gleeful about traveling on an ocean liner to a new world. Unlike her daughter, Hannah Klein had been sad and afraid. She'd hated leaving her husband and sons, Simon and David, but when the emigration papers arrived her father insisted that they go to America.

Luckily, Molly had her friend Cleo, who was smart and funny, but Mama, stuck in the store with Uncle Abe, was sad much of the time. Only the letters that came every week from Swidnik lightened the gloom.

Where is Uncle Abe, she wondered again, frowning at the small cloud of feathers that rose as she brushed her hand across the counter. He fussed about making the store look nicer, but how that was possible in his messy business she could never understand.

The bell over the door chimed and Molly looked up to see a customer very different from those who usually came to Klein's Poultry Store. Instead of a housewife wearing a black shawl over her plain gray dress, she saw a young woman in a crisp white shirtwaist and trim black skirt that barely brushed her ankles. Her hair was gathered into a neat bun atop her head and her gray-blue eyes were bright with curiosity.

"Do you work here?" she said, her words clear and precise, no hint of an accent in her speech. Unlike most of the people in the boarding house where Molly and her mother lived and the customers who frequented the store, this was no immigrant.

"Sometimes, ma'am," Molly answered. She didn't know what to make of this woman who looked and sounded so different from other adults.

"What do you mean, sometimes? You either work here or you don't."

"I help out when my mother can't be here or my uncle is away," Molly said.

"They should encourage you to speak up, so your customers can understand what you're saying," the woman replied.

Molly's face felt hot. She tried to speak proper English. She and Mama practiced together. Her mother said she did fine, that she sounded like a real American, not a greenhorn like Hannah. And Cleo, who was born in Alabama, understood everything she said. Did this lady mean she couldn't understand Molly's English?

"No need to frown like that. I'm trying to tell you not to speak so softly. If you address others confidently they'll respect you more and accept what you tell them."

She smiled and Molly felt better; the lady had straight white teeth and looked friendlier when she was smiling.

"Are your mother and uncle the owners of this store?"

Molly shook her head. "Only my uncle. My mother has worked for him since we came from Poland."

"I see. When was that?"

"A little over three years ago. The rest of my family is still there, but we hope they'll get out soon."

She couldn't tell this person with so many questions about the wrenching decision to split her family. Papa, trying so hard to be cheerful, had tried to comfort them.

"We'll follow you soon, don't worry. Abe could only sponsor two of our family for now and I must stay here and find someone to take over the shop. The boys will help me, we'll save our money, and, before you know it, we'll all be together."

Molly remembered how Papa had held Mama in his arms as she wept and protested.

"It has to be this way, Hannah. You know life in Swidnik is not good anymore. The farmers are so poor they can't afford the coats and trousers from my tailoring shop and our customers in town aren't much better off. In America, we'll have a wonderful new life. People will order fancy clothes and I'll be the most successful tailor in Pittsburgh. You and Molly will wear only silks and fine woolens and the boys will have a dozen velvet vests!"

Her brothers had rolled their eyes and Mama laughed, drying her tears. Her father could always make them laugh, Molly thought. If Uncle Abe tried that instead of gruffness she'd be more comfortable with him.

Whenever she began to feel settled in her new country, one overwhelming fear drew her thoughts back to Poland—to her father and brothers.

Molly didn't tell anyone—not even Cleo—how scared she was for them. At any time the Polish police could decide the Jews were the town's troublemakers. It didn't matter if they were honest shopkeepers minding their own businesses, trying to take care of their families. The police could storm in, arrest them for invented crimes, use any excuse to beat them.

What if her father was one of their victims, before he and the boys could come to America? Molly tried to free her mind from the horrid thoughts, forcing herself to concentrate on the woman demanding her attention.

The visitor was watching her. "Since your uncle isn't here, perhaps you can help me. I'm writing an article for my hometown newspaper in Nebraska about chicken cellars and I understand there's one below this poultry store."

Molly's bafflement overcame her shyness with this bold American woman.

"Chicken cellar? I'm sorry, but I don't understand."

"Of course you do," she answered, her impatience creating small furrows between her eyes. "Your uncle raises his own chickens, does he not, in the basement? I imagine those steps at the back lead down there."

This woman wanted to see the place where Uncle Abe kept the chickens he sold to his customers! Molly hated going down there. The stink of all the droppings, the dust and the terrible air made her cough. Her eyes burned every time she was sent down to replenish their feed or bring them more water and her throat hurt so that she could hardly breathe. She didn't know how her mother could stand going to the cellar every day. Molly was certain her uncle wouldn't want strangers down there scaring the chickens and creating a commotion.

"I'm sorry, Ma'am, but customers aren't supposed to go down there. My uncle wouldn't like it."

"Oh, bother your uncle. If he asks, tell him he has nothing to fear from me. My name's Willa Cather and I'm not really a customer. I've been living in Pittsburgh since I took a job here after college. I send stories about some of my experiences to a newspaper back in Lincoln, Nebraska, where I attended the university."

Molly listened, fascinated. She'd never met anyone from the West, where she thought only cowboys lived.

"People back there would be interested in reading about subterranean chicken houses, especially the farmers in my part of the country. Explain to your uncle that his store will be famous in Nebraska and I'm sure he won't mind."

Having finished what she considered a reasonable explanation, she moved to the back of the store and started toward the stairs before Molly could stop her. Rushing to catch up, Molly went down the steps behind her, calling, "These are very steep. Please, be careful."

Miss Cather had pulled a folded white handkerchief from the cuff of her long-sleeved blouse and was holding it to her nose.

"Phew! What a stench. How do you stand it?"

"Mama says you can get used to anything," Molly said, placing her feet carefully on the slimy, feather-littered floor.

Her companion turned and looked at her.

"Yes, I suppose that's so. What's your name, young lady?"

"Molly. Molly Klein."

"Don't worry about my being here, Molly. If your uncle complains, tell him I insisted, because that's what journalists do, and he won't blame you."

Molly wasn't at all sure of that, but it was certainly true she couldn't stop Miss Cather, who stared, wide-eyed, at her surroundings. She'd put her handkerchief back in her cuff so that she could write in a small notebook.

The visitor looked at the piles of feed and the water pans scattered through the cellar and at the roosts where clusters of hens, disturbed by the intruders, clucked noisily and flapped their wings.

"How many chickens does your uncle keep here?" she asked, raising her voice to be heard above the din.

"I don't know," Molly said. She thought there were more than a hundred, but she'd decided the less she said, the better.

Miss Cather looked at the walls made of earth, with small caves cut into the dirt, where the hens roosted. She peered at the chicks scratching in the soil.

"Are these chicks hatched here?"

"I think so," Molly answered.

"Do the poor fowls ever see any light?"

Molly shrugged. She didn't like to think about the baby chicks, always shrouded in darkness, any more than she liked to think about the grown birds, the veins in their necks severed so they could provide meals for people's tables. Her mother said that feeding families was more important than worrying about chickens raised for that purpose, but Molly always tried to be away from the store when the hens were slaughtered.

"Apparently, only your uncle can answer my questions. I think I've seen enough. Let's go back upstairs."

Miss Cather held up the hem of her skirt as they ascended the stairs, speaking words that Molly knew were meant more for herself than as conversation.

"I shall tell my readers how tiny birds are hatched and grow in cellars, laying their eggs in Stygian blackness surrounded by damp, sick-smelling earth. Truly appalling, like something out of the Dark Ages."

Back in the store, the visitor tucked her notebook and pencil into her skirt pocket and again pulled out her handkerchief to dab at her forehead and upper lip. When she'd finished she looked around, then directed her attention to a nervous Molly.

"Goodbye, Molly Klein. I doubt we'll meet again, but if you tell your uncle about my being here you should also tell him that I insisted upon going down to the chicken cellar and you had nothing to do with it."

Then she turned and left the store, the door banging behind her.

TWO

"Whew!" Molly breathed a deep sigh of relief and sat down on the stool behind the counter, wondering how to tell her uncle about Willa Cather's visit.

The bell above the entrance chimed again and Uncle Abe strode in. A burly man, not very tall, but stocky and muscular, he had a raspy voice that matched his temperament.

"So, Molly, it's good you can sit there like a lady without a care in the world. Did you sweep and straighten up the store like I asked?"

"Yes, Uncle Abe."

"Good. Any business while I was gone?"

Molly hesitated. Business meant customers and Miss Cather wasn't that. She wouldn't be lying if she didn't mention her.

"Mrs. Stein bought a dozen eggs. Nobody came for chickens."

He shook his head, then rubbed his hand across the gray stubble on his face. "Some days I don't know how I can afford to pay the bills. Good thing Harry Kramer, down the street, gave me a nice order for hens and eggs to take to his brother's store in Johnstown or we might all be starving, like in the old country."

"We always had enough food to eat in Swidnik. Papa made sure of that."

Molly had to stop herself from shouting at him about how hard her mother worked in the poultry store for the tiny wage he paid her. Mama insisted she must never criticize Uncle Abe, who'd been responsible for bringing them to this country, finding a place for them to live, and giving Mama a job.

Still, Molly thought that he didn't appreciate her mother's gentle, uncomplaining manner. A widower, he lived alone above the store, in rooms crowded with heavy mahogany furniture and hand-painted china. She and Mama shared a cramped bedroom in a boarding house that was always noisy, stuffy and hot in summer and so drafty in winter they wore sweaters and scarves when they went to the dining room for their dinner.

If Cleo didn't live next door Molly knew she would despise the place, so different from the home she'd shared with her parents and brothers in Poland.

In Swidnik, she'd had her own small room, while her brothers shared a larger alcove near the kitchen. There was a patch of garden where Mama picked big white radishes, sweet carrots, and the fragrant dill she used to make pickles that smelled of garlic and brine.

There were other girls to play with, at least for a while. Miriam's family had left for America before she and Mama emigrated. Rose's father went to Canada and sent money back for the rest of them. She and Rose had said tearful goodbyes at the train station.

In their town many of the men had left for America or Canada, planning to find work and then send for their families. Their neighbors were surprised when Papa insisted she and Mama leave first, to be with his uncle in Pittsburgh. When Abe had explained he couldn't arrange for all of them to come together Papa decided he and the boys should stay and try to find somebody to take over his business; Mama's health would be better in America and Molly, their youngest, must go with her.

Molly said goodbye to Uncle Abe and hurried along Fulton Street to meet Cleo. Things hadn't worked out as Molly's parents hoped. After more than three years, the business was still not sold. Papa and the boys hadn't yet saved enough money to come to America and, as far as she could tell, her mother's health hadn't improved. She was much too thin and pale, often so tired at the end of a day in the store that she crept into bed without eating anything.

Some nights Molly was awakened by her mother's soft sobs. She knew Hannah was lonely for Papa and the boys, but there was nothing Molly could do about it. She never mentioned those tearful episodes because she thought her mother needed to believe they were private sorrows.

"What took you so long?" Cleo was waving and shouting from the corner where the streetcar stopped. "Hurry up, slowpoke, or we'll never get to the park."

Molly smiled, forgetting her annoyance at Uncle Abe. Cleo, not much taller than her friend, seemed so because she was so slender, all gangly arms and legs. Her skin was light brown—"coffee with cream" she called it—and her delicate nose was sprinkled with darker freckles. Her hair, in two fat braids, wound around her head, anchored by a bright red bow. Molly wished her hair was thick and dramatic like Cleo's, instead of short and straight, with bangs marching in line across her forehead. Her mother cut her hair, insisting it looked fine, no matter how much Molly complained.

"Sorry to be late," Molly said as she joined her friend. "I had to stay in the store until my uncle finally came back and it took him a long time. While he was out I had a strange visit from a lady who wanted to see the cellar where the chickens are raised."

Cleo's eyes widened. "That's peculiar, all right. Did you take her down?"

"I couldn't stop her, she just pushed her way."

Molly described her experience as they waited for the streetcar, ignoring the din of the busy street and the flow of people around them. They sidestepped the pushcarts of grunting peddlers, their wagons heavy with everything from cabbages and apples to boys' pants and ladies' aprons.

Among the men hurrying past, some wore the white jackets and black trousers of waiters hurrying to their jobs in hotel dining rooms. A few bit into chunks of rye bread from loaves they carried in brown wrapping paper. Women in groups of two or three moved more slowly, some speaking in Polish or Russian that Molly recognized, others in the rapid, lilting notes she knew to be Italian. Lacking market baskets, they carried their purchases of cabbages, potatoes, and cauliflowers bundled in their aprons. A few had live chickens, which Molly hoped they'd bought from Uncle Abe. The hens peeked out of brown butcher's paper.

Once, when she and Cleo were walking home, they'd seen a chicken escape from a woman's bundle and hop down the sidewalk. Its owner had screamed and begun chasing it, swearing in a language the girls didn't understand, while the potatoes and apples she was carrying fell from her apron and rolled into the street. Molly, Cleo and some passersby joined the chase and Cleo caught the hen. Holding it by its neck and trying to avoid its snapping beak and wildly beating wings, she'd returned it to its grateful owner. Later, the girls sat down on the curb and laughed until their sides ached.

"Did you remember to bring a lunch?" Cleo asked.

Molly groaned. "I was in such a hurry to get to the store—Mama was worried Uncle Abe'd be mad that she couldn't come in—I forgot."

"Never mind. I have enough for both of us. My daddy brought leftovers home from the hotel last night. Chicken, tomatoes, even chocolate cake. When he works the late dinner shift we always get treats. There's probably enough for Vittorio—pardon me, Victor—too."

They heard the clang of the streetcar coming along the tracks, dropped their pennies into the fare box and hurried to the back of the car where they could sit near a window. They liked the ride to the park through streets that followed the river. Along the river's shore vast steel mills belched flames and thick black smoke, staining the air around them orange and gray with soot and gritty particles of coal.

The girls looked at the houses lining the streets, speculating about the families living behind windows hung with grimy white curtains fluttering in the breeze raised by the speeding trolley. Molly guessed that the curtains were washed and ironed every-day to stay clean in the filth of the city. Often, they'd see people sitting on porches and wave to them as they passed. Occasionally, they heard the sounds of pianos or organs coming through the open windows.

"My daddy would like to own a good piano more than any-thing. Granny says our old, beat-up one belongs on the gar-bage heap. You should hear him play ragtime, Molly. He's so good. When he was my age, down south, Daddy used to play in churches and at parties and earn money he'd bring home and put away in a cigar box. He was saving to come up north and have a fine, new life. Granny says he'd be famous if he had more time for his music."

"What's ragtime? I never heard of that in Swidnik."

Cleo laughed. "I guess not. It's a special music that colored people know, with a regular rhythm and then a melody you sort of play with. 'Embellish' is the word my daddy uses. It's hard to explain, but you'd understand if you heard it."

Molly looked at her friend. "I'd like to. Maybe he could play it and get paid, so he wouldn't need to wash dishes at the hotel anymore."

"That's what I told him," Cleo answered, her face solemn. "But he said other Negroes are as poor as we are and most can't afford to go to places to listen to music and the same's true for the white folks who work in the hotels and the stores. Sometimes he plays in a club on the Hill, not far from our boarding house. But it's mostly just for fun." She smiled. "You know how he likes to joke. The last time I asked him about playing, he said he hadn't gotten an invitation yet to perform at one of Mr. Andrew Carnegie's parties. Or his libraries, either."

Molly pointed to a porch they were passing, where two boys who looked about their age sat on wicker chairs that must once have been white but were now the color of storm clouds. They wore collarless shirts and trousers covered with smudges that matched the chairs; both were laughing as they plucked at banjos cradled in their laps.

"They probably won't be entertaining Mr. Carnegie's guests either, but look how much fun they're having," Molly said.

Cleo nodded. "Having a good time makes the work go easier. That's what Granny says."

"She does seem to, even when she's scrubbing the floor. I always feel better when I'm around your grandmother. Hearing her laugh makes me laugh, too," Molly said.

She studied her friend's profile as the streetcar rattled its way along the tracks. Cleo's high forehead with its fringe of springy black curls, her delicate nose and generous mouth with its cleft above the upper lip, made her look, Molly thought, like one of the sculptures in the big Hall of Statues at the museum.

Last year, when her class went there on a field trip, Cleo had posed between two of them, hiding her arms behind her because the statues' arms were missing. Body stiff, feet pointed, she'd made their classmates laugh. The sounds echoed through the vast room until their teacher shushed them and made them move on. Molly was jolted out of that memory by the streetcar's jerking stop. Each time it picked up more passengers, the others braced their bodies to keep from lurching forward.

"Do you think she misses Alabama? Or that your father does?" Molly asked.

"They don't talk about it much," Cleo answered. "Granny says life up here's easier for her because she doesn't have to work so hard tending to crops and animals. I guess she misses her relatives, but she doesn't complain."

"Neither does my mother, but at night, when she thinks I'm asleep, she cries. If my father and brothers would get here she'd finally be happy in America."

"Shucks, my folks have always been in America and I don't know as that makes them any happier."

Her friend's comment encouraged Molly to ask the question she'd always wondered about. "Do you miss your mother, Cleo?"

Her companion's shoulders contracted in a shrug.

"Child, I hardly knew her. I can't remember what she looked like even if I try." She looked down at her hands, clasped in her lap. "Sometimes I think about her, though, and try to understand why she left Daddy and me. When I was younger I used to ask him and he'd answer that she was so sad and fault-finding she had to go looking for her happiness. He'd say when I was older I'd understand how that happens with some people."

Cleo turned to look at Molly, her eyes hard, without their usual brightness.

"But I don't and I never will, no matter how old I get to be. She didn't care about us or she never would've left Daddy and me. He said she had a beautiful voice and wanted to be a singer and see the world. Maybe her voice was beautiful but her heart was ugly or she wouldn't have run away from her husband and her baby."

Usually full of jokes and laughter, a silent Cleo turned to stare out the window. Molly was sorry she'd brought the subject up and didn't know what to say to make her friend feel better.

She looked around the increasingly crowded streetcar. Ladies carrying heavy parcels squeezed close together on the bench-like side seats. At each stop more people poured in. Soon, even with the windows open, the car was filled with the mingled smells of ripe produce and perspiring bodies crushed close together.

The heat of the July day made the air worse and Molly began to feel queasy. Her uncle said that over 400,000 people lived in Pittsburgh now. To her, it felt like all of them were trying to pack themselves into the streetcar.

Cleo nudged her. "The next stop's ours. Get ready to push your way off."

To Molly's relief, they finally squeezed out past the mass of people and hurried to the entrance to Schenley Park. She inhaled deeply.

Cleo, doing the same, said, "These flowers are perfume after that streetcar. But we can't just stand around breathing all day. Let's go look for Victor at the fountain."

THREE

Along a path shaded by oak trees, the girls walked to a massive concrete pool filled with water, a statue rising from its center. They didn't know what the figure represented, but it looked important, spouting glistening streams of water into the basin. People clustered around the pool, enjoying the spray and trailing their fingers through the cool water. Trouser legs rolled up to their knees, boys chased each other around the statue, splashing the adults who sat on the fountain's rim. Nobody complained, grateful for temporary relief from the day's heat. Sitting among them, shoes off and feet swinging, was their friend, Vittorio Morelli. He waved, signaling to them to take off their shoes and join him.

"Why so late?" he said when they were close enough to hear him above the racket. "I thought I'd have to wade alone. Did you bring lunches?"

Cleo held up her bag and they sat on either side of him.

"I was on time but Molly poked around in the store. I thought we'd never get here." Cleo was pulling off her shoes and stockings as she spoke. "Ah, perfect," she sighed as the water lapped her ankles. "If those pesky kids don't step on my feet I'll stay here forever. Lily pads will grow between my toes and little frogs can hop right on over them. Molly, don't you want to get your feet wet?"

Molly shook her head. She could feel the big toe of her left foot through a hole in her stocking and she didn't want the others to see. She'd mend it tonight. Mama couldn't afford to buy more stockings just now. She bent over to trail her fingers through the water.

"Vittorio, where've you been? We haven't seen you much lately."

"Victor, Molly. Get it right. Vittorio sounds like some greenhorn from the old country. It's bad enough my relatives call me that and refuse to talk to me in English, pretending they don't understand what I'm saying. They conveniently forget I was born right here in Pittsburgh. To them, we still live in Italy and they don't want me to get too American and give up the old ways. It feels like I spend half my time arguing with my family."

His eyes reminded Molly of a black velvet dress her mother used to wear in Swidnik.

"Are you going to be cranky today?" Cleo asked. "If so, I'm taking my shoes and lunch and finding another space where people are cheerier. Molly's complaining about nosy customers, you're mad at your relatives—must be the heat."

Victor laughed.

"I'm always mad at my relatives. Except Uncle Gino, who's teaching me to play his violin. Did some of my nosy family come into your uncle's store?"

Molly shook her head, smiling.

"This woman spoke English. Correct English. Everything about her was *so* correct."

She described the incident while Cleo wiggled her feet in the pool, sometimes kicking water at the young boys who ran past. They grinned at her and splashed back.

Although Victor lived several blocks away from their boarding houses, the three of them had become friends when they were in the same class at school. Sometimes the girls had helped Victor with homework assignments because, at the beginning of the year, he was still having trouble with the language.

As the term progressed he'd become better in English and showed special talent in math. Soon, he was moved into an advanced math class and helped Cleo and Molly, much less skillful at numbers, with their homework. Like his friends, his teachers were impressed with his math aptitude, encouraging him to take college preparatory classes.

"I won't be able to work as much in the store when we start Central High in the fall," Molly said, concluding her story about Miss Cather's visit. "Mama understands, but Uncle Abe talks about how, when he was fifteen, he left school and his home in Poland and made his own way until he came to Pittsburgh and started his business. He brags about how he earned a living and supported a wife without going to high school, but my mother always answers that I have to graduate. It's not easy for her to stand up to him, but on that subject, she does."

Molly sighed and patted water on her face. "When school starts she'll have to work even harder." She looked at her hands. White petals, carried by a hot breeze, had fallen into the fountain and were clinging to her wet fingers.

"At least she stands up to him," Victor said. "All my relatives would agree with your uncle. They don't want me to go back to school. His brothers keep telling my father it's time I learn the stone masonry trade. They've got a big job coming up, fixing cobblestones along some streetcar tracks. Good money, they keep saying, and my father's beginning to listen."

"His *paesanos* think so, too. 'Boys shoulda be workin', bringin' home money to help the family, not sittin' in little chairs, scratchin' numbers on papers nobody looks at but olda maid teachers.'"

Victor was such a good mimic that people near them heard and laughed.

He didn't think it was funny. Molly and Cleo knew how much he wanted to learn more math. Sometimes he talked about attending college and studying to become a mathematician.

Cleo swung her legs over the rim of the fountain and shook her feet, scattering droplets of water.

"Let's go up to Flagstaff Hill and eat. My stomach's growling louder than Victor's relatives."

"Does it sound like I'm complaining?" Victor asked, standing quickly so that he splashed Molly's face. It felt good, temporary relief from the burning sun. "I'm telling you my troubles. Isn't that what friends are for?"

"This friend likes it better when you tell funny stories about your family," Cleo answered, walking so fast the others raced to keep up.

"Slow down," Molly said. "It's too hot to rush. Victor can't walk this fast and think up funny stories."

He looked down at Molly. Victor was nearly six feet tall, towering above the girls.

"You doubt my mental abilities, Miss Klein? Let me tell you about numbers." He started singing the multiplication tables while the girls groaned. "And that's justa what I learned my first week in night school," he finished in a thick accent. When his friends laughed, he explained, "My Uncle Gino. He's my favorite."

They walked across the grass on Flagstaff Hill and sat down beneath a cluster of trees. The grass felt cool and smelled freshly cut. A slight breeze stirred the leaves overhead, their rustle soft background music as they talked.

"He's the one teaching you to play the violin?" Molly said.

"Yes. You should hear him. He's good. Plays Neapolitan street songs that make the old ladies cry. Or else they sing, which is worse! Uncle Gino says I'm slow but I have a good ear, so there's hope for me."

Victor bit into a sandwich he took from his bag. It was thicker than any Molly had ever seen. Part of a loaf of bread was split across the middle and filled with chunks of hard-boiled eggs, tomatoes, onions, peppers, and sliced meat. The bread glistened with olive oil and was speckled with parsley. The sandwich smelled spicy and delicious.

"I'll never play like my uncle," Victor said. "But that's all right. It's fun and I even have a job on Sunday."

Cleo looked up from the chicken leg she'd been carefully unwrapping. "A job? For money? You're joking, right?"

"No joke. I'm going to play with Uncle Gino and some of his friends at a party on Centre Avenue. The *paesanos* from Abruzzi are getting together to sing, eat, drink *vino*, and talk about the old country. The food will be good and so will the stories. And I'll earn a couple of bucks."

Molly had finished the sandwich she'd gotten from Cleo and was about to start an apple. She looked at Victor.

"Abruzzi? *Paesanos*? Sometimes I don't know what you're talking about, like you're speaking another language."

"I am," he said, laughing. "Abruzzi is a part of Italy that lots of people who settled in Pittsburgh came from. Most of them belong to what's called a Beneficial Society—like a club, where they try to help each other find jobs, meet other Italians, stuff like that. When they come from the same place they call each other *paesano*. It's like a buddy or cousin, except they may not be related." He wiped his hand across his mouth, then looked into his empty lunch bag to see if he'd overlooked anything. "It's hard to explain. Anyhow, the Beneficial Society's having a party on Sunday. Uncle Gino, some other guys and me will play."

"I", said Cleo.

Vic looked at her, puzzled.

"Uncle Gino, some other guys, and I," she explained.

"You and Gino, the star pupils," he answered. "Just don't sing the multiplication tables."

Molly wanted to stop what sounded like the beginning of bickering between her friends. They sometimes did it and seemed to enjoy it, like a game, but it reminded her too much of the way Uncle Abe acted with her mother.

"What I don't understand," she said, "is how you'll play your uncle's violin if he's there, too. What'll you do, take turns passing it back and forth?"

Victor smiled. "After a few *grappas*—strong wine to you two foreigners—the people at the party probably wouldn't notice. But Uncle Gino's borrowing another fiddle from a friend."

"So what will the friend use?" Cleo said. "A tin can and a spoon?"

"Something much better. An accordion," Victor answered. "You ever hear one of those squeeze boxes? Very mellow."

Molly rubbed her apple against the sleeve of her dress, then bit into it. "I guess it would sound better than a can and a spoon. Even an extra-large size can."

They stood, brushing grass clippings from their clothes.

"Let's walk awhile before we get a streetcar back to the Hill," Cleo said. "The air smells so much better here."

"But it doesn't smell at all," Victor said.

"That's the idea, you genius of multiplication tables," Cleo answered.

They walked down the grassy slope, talking and laughing. Not necessarily aware of their city's reputation as America's leading steel producer, the three friends, like the immigrants crowded together in the Hill District, were only too familiar with the effects of heavy industry. As smoke and soot from the mountains of soft coal needed to fuel the steel mills, the aluminum and glass factories, and the trains, drifted over the city, they endured the results.

Pastel clothes and curtains turned gray. Thick, sticky layers of black dust settled on every surface no matter how often it was dusted away. Sometimes, weeks passed when the sun's rays barely penetrated the noon darkness. At school, classmates with pale, sickly faces coughed endlessly into their dirty handkerchiefs.

Molly thought about some of Uncle Abe's customers, unmarried men employed in the mills. They would buy a chicken for Sunday dinner and coax their boarding house landladies to cook it for them. Molly shuddered when she heard them describe the way they lived, crowded into shabby rooms where their beds were used in double shifts, night and day. Sometimes, when their shift times changed, they had to sleep on the floor because other men were in their beds.

Once she'd overheard a customer complaining to her mother about the foremen and how superior they acted to the immigrants. "He was talking to a friend, another boss, and they laughed at us, said we'd work for less money than the others because we don't know any better. Just give us rye bread, a herring and beer, he said, like we're too stupid to want anything more."

Mama looked sad but both she and the customer knew he'd keep working for his hateful boss. He had no other choice.

At least in America, Molly reminded herself, the mill worker couldn't be put in jail because he was different, and from another country. In Swidnik, her father and his friends could be dragged away, arrested and beaten because they were Jewish. In the Poland she'd left, their religion was reason enough to abuse them. She tried yet again to push the sick fear out of her mind.

One of her mother's favorites was Herb Collins, a colored man who drove a freight wagon and often came in to visit. Herb and Uncle Abe were old friends; he'd sometimes worked in the store before Molly and her mother arrived in Pittsburgh.

"Hey, Abe, how you doin'?" he'd call out as he sauntered in. "And Missus Hannah, my favorite sweet lady. How are you, sweetheart? Not lettin' that loudmouth uncle fuss at you? He do that, you tell me, sugar, and I'll fix him, hear? I'll hide his smelly old cigars!"

Sometimes, around the holidays, when they were busier than usual Herb would still get behind the counter to weigh the chickens and cut them up for customers. Molly admired the deft way he'd wrap the tan butcher's paper around the fowls' awkward shapes and quickly tie the bundle with white cord he pulled from the spool hanging above the register. He'd hand the package to the customer with a broad smile and a big thank-you.

Herb said he liked driving his wagon all over the Hill, getting to talk to people when he picked up and delivered freight. He'd grown up on a farm in Georgia so he enjoyed caring for the big mare he'd named Flora, who pulled his wagon up the steep hills and along the crooked streets of the city. Herb told Uncle Abe he usually worked ten hours a day and earned twelve dollars a week. Most of what he earned he sent back to his family in Georgia. When Mama asked if he wasn't lonely so far away from them he explained he planned to buy a farm in the country where they'd all be together, even Flora.

Molly was surprised by Cleo's reaction when she told her friend about Herb's plan.

"He's sure different from my daddy, who'd never want to do that. My grandpa was a sharecropper working all his life to grow other people's crops. Granny says he was a tired old man when he died at 42. I guess that's why my father wants to work in the steel mill, where he can make more money than at the hotel or by picking up a few music jobs."

"I thought he liked playing the piano best of all," Molly had said.

"He does, but he says it won't put bread on the table or pretty dresses on me."

Making a living preoccupied everyone in Molly's life: Papa in the old country; Mama here, trying to put aside a few dollars each month to help bring their family to America; Victor's relatives, urging him to quit school and go to work.

They left Schenley Park. Cleo, Victor and Molly boarded a streetcar to go back to their neighborhood, sitting together on the long, bench-like seats at the front of the car.

"When I get paid for playing at the party with my uncle and his friends," said Victor, "I'm going to keep some of the money and treat you both to something special."

"Like what?" Cleo asked.

"And how will you keep the money? Your father'll expect you to give it to him," Molly added.

"He won't know if I hold back a few dollars. If I earn it I should decide what to do with it."

Cleo said, "You don't have the money yet. Granny would say you shouldn't count your chicks before they're hatched."

"Not chickens again," Molly complained. "I've heard more than enough about them already today."

The others laughed. Cleo coaxed Victor to describe the treat he promised, but he refused, saying only, "You're gonna like it."

He got off the streetcar first, turning to give them a jaunty salute before disappearing around a corner.

Molly and Cleo got off together and walked slowly to their boarding houses, trying to make the afternoon last a little longer.

"I won't see you till next week," Cleo said as they parted. "Granny and I'll be busy with church and you'll probably be helping in the store most of the time."

Molly nodded.

"I'll go in before lunchtime, so Mama can come home and rest a few hours. She likes to practice reading and writing English then, too, and she's making some clothes for me to wear to school in the fall."

"I bet she likes that better than working in that hot, stuffy store," Cleo said. "Lordy, I declare I don't know how she can stand it. Maybe she should take up dressmaking."

"She does like to sew, but she'd earn even less at that than she does now. People around here can't afford to hire someone to make their clothes. Sometimes Mama sews to help out, like the skirts she made for the Korman children when their mother got sick. She stayed up late at night to do it and was so tired the next day she could hardly go to work."

Molly looked at Cleo. "I'm not going to let that happen to me. I'll go to school, get a good job, and take care of Mama."

They were standing in front of Cleo's building.

"Listen to the child," Cleo said. "Fifteen years old and her whole life's planned. Okay, Miss Molly, tell me how you're gonna be rich and famous and support your family."

"I'll finish high school, go to college. Maybe be a teacher. Then I'll get a good job in a school like Central High, get summers off to travel and do whatever I like."

Cleo's eyebrows lifted. "You probably could be a teacher— you're bossy enough to order a room full of kids around. Especially if they're first and second graders and shorter than you."

"I'm trying to be serious. Do I make fun of you because you're so skinny and trip over your own feet?"

Cleo grinned. "Remember how shy you were when you first came from Poland? Like a skittery mouse, not wanting to talk because you couldn't speak anything but that funny babble I couldn't understand. What was it called again?"

"Yiddish. It's a language, not babble. And I knew some English. My father made us all study it," Molly said.

"Right. And you nagged me to practice with you until I finally could figure out what you were saying. Now you're so sassy I was better off when you were a mouse."

"Squeak, squeak. You haven't said what you think about my idea."

"About going to college? You're smart, you'd work hard, and you've got a lot of ambition."

"But?" said Molly, noticing her friend's hesitation.

"I don't know how you can do it," Cleo said, her face serious now. "It costs a lot of money and your family can't pay that. Your Uncle Abe probably wouldn't be thrilled, either."

"He can fly away with his chickens! My parents would be proud of me. I could work, get a job to help pay the tuition."

"You'd have to work so many hours you wouldn't have time left to go to school."

"I'm strong. I know I could do both. And I will, you'll see." Her voice had risen loudly enough to attract the attention of passersby, who turned to look.

"Hey, I'm your friend, remember. You don't have to convince me how stubborn you are. I better go inside or Granny will threaten to tan my hide. See you in a few days."

Molly seldom talked about her plans, even to Cleo, but she thought about them nearly all the time. She couldn't stand to live this way forever, with the stink of chickens in her nostrils, and streets so dark and smelly they might as well live in a cellar. Mama would scold if she knew her thoughts and remind Molly again of how lucky they were to live in America. But this wasn't the country everyone in Swidnik dreamed about. Their America had flowers, green grass everywhere and big white houses that gleamed in the sun. Nothing here gleamed: the sun was sickly and weak, like so many of the children—like her own mother. She'd work hard and find another, brighter place for her family. She had to!

Molly waved goodbye and went next door. She walked up the cracked concrete stairs and across the small porch with its peeling paint into the hall of the boarding house where she and Mama shared a room. The hallway was dim and musty, the hot air smelling of dust and stale cooking. She climbed two flights of stairs to the corner room beneath the attic.

Crammed into the small space was a bed, a chest with four drawers and a sink. The battered table, whose peeling top and two chairs had once been painted blue, was where Molly did schoolwork and her mother read, sewed, or wrote letters to her husband and sons. An old sewing machine that had belonged to Uncle Abe's wife took up most of the remaining space.

Hannah Klein looked up from a letter she was reading and smiled at her daughter. Molly noticed that the skin around her mother's eyes looked pink, her nose slightly reddened, as if she'd been crying.

People thought her mother was beautiful; she had soft, wavy black hair that she pulled back in a bun, but curly tendrils escaped and framed an oval face with high cheekbones and large, thickly fringed green eyes. In the years since she'd left most of her family thousands of miles across the ocean, Hannah's pale skin had developed tiny lines near her eyes and mouth. There were hollows under her cheekbones and dark shadows beneath her eyes. Her mother looked frailer than she had when they'd left Poland. She laughed less and, although she tried to hide it, was often sad.

Molly sympathized, but was sometimes impatient. Certainly Hannah missed her family; so did she. But Papa was doing everything he could to join them and, meantime, the two of them were in a new country with many opportunities. Molly wanted her mother to be happier about their new life and thought she should try harder. She pushed away those thoughts because they pricked her conscience. Maybe she wasn't helping enough; her brothers would do better if they were here.

"Did you enjoy yourself, Malke, in the park with your friends?" her mother asked.

"Molly, Mama. You must speak English and use my English name. We agreed, remember?"

Her mother's hands twisted together as she shifted in the chair, which creaked even under her slight weight. "It's hard. Sometimes I think if I stop using our own language it will be one more part of home I have to give up."

"Home is here, in America, now. That's what Papa wanted for us."

"I know. But without him and the boys . . ."

She didn't finish, but Molly know what she was thinking. She took her mother's hand, pressing the thin fingers against her sturdier ones. "It will be all right, Mama, you'll see. When Papa and my brothers are here with us, you'll feel like we're all, finally, home."

Hannah Klein smiled at her daughter, but her eyes glistened with unshed tears.

FOUR

Molly tried to remember how hard her mother's life was without good friends to help, the way Cleo and Victor helped her.

"You're doing fine with English. Doesn't Miss Bauman at the Settlement House say that?"

Hannah nodded.

"She's a nice lady and helps all the foreigners. What we learn in class I try at the store, but the language is hard. I get mixed up and I feel so—so stupid."

"Everybody gets mixed up about something, even the Americans. Cleo's really smart, but she has trouble with math. Victor helps her, the way Miss Bauman helps you."

Her mother smiled, but Molly could see she was thinking about something else.

"What did you do after class today?" she asked Hannah. "You should go for a walk or visit some neighbors when you aren't working. Not sit cooped up in this hot room."

"I was writing to Papa and the boys, answering the letter that came earlier. It's on the table."

"Why don't you tell me about it and I'll read it later."

Her mother looked down, avoiding Molly's eyes. Molly knew she was fighting tears.

"Things are the same. They're working hard and trying to find someone interested in our little business. Uncle Herschel sent his friend from a town about fifty kilometers away. Papa said the man liked Swidnik but couldn't afford the store. They're still talking about it, but your father thinks nothing will happen."

She looked at Molly, eyes teary.

"I am so afraid, always afraid that Papa and your brothers will never be able to come here."

Her anguish poured out in a burst of Yiddish, but Molly didn't remind her of her promise. Her mother was too troubled to remember about speaking English.

"Papa will find a way. You have to be strong and believe that, Mama. If you got sick or sounded hopeless in your letters, think how terrible he would feel."

Hannah wiped her eyes with a handkerchief trimmed in lace that she'd crocheted in Poland. She tucked it into her sleeve. "You're right. I'm lucky to have such a smart daughter. Tell me about the park and your friends. Then we must get ready to go to Bella Bloom's place. She's invited us and Uncle Abe to dinner."

Molly made a face, knowing that she and Hannah provided an excuse for Mrs. Bloom to pursue Uncle Abe. A plump immigrant from Russia, she and her husband came to the Hill soon after Uncle Abe and his wife, Rose, settled there. Neither couple had children; they'd often visited together, playing cards and gossiping.

Now that both were widowed, Molly thought anyone could see that Mrs. Bloom was after Uncle Abe. She wore shiny black dresses and too much rouge and her fat, stubby fingers were adorned with heavy gold rings. When she was bored with the adults' conversation Molly would amuse herself watching Mrs. Bloom's chins wobbling as she spoke.

On their way to dinner, Hannah bought flowers Molly knew she couldn't afford. Her mother insisted it was the polite thing to do. When their hostess urged them to a table crowded with flower-patterned dishes, heavy crystal glasses, and a tall decanter of sweet red wine, Molly helped Mrs. Bloom bring bowls of steaming soup and platters of boiled beef with noodles to the table. She wondered how their hostess could move so quickly in a dress threatening to split at the seams.

Uncle Abe was talkative and good-humored during their evenings with Mrs. Bloom. She always had his favorite wine and cigars for him to smoke after dinner.

Walking home later, Molly asked her mother if she thought Abe would marry Mrs. Bloom. "I don't know why she bothers to invite us, she's so busy flattering him and refilling his plate with that greasy food she's so proud of preparing. She asks how we are, but she doesn't wait for an answer or listen to what we say."

"You shouldn't talk like that, it isn't nice," her mother said, but Molly knew she agreed.

"Bella's neighbors would gossip if Uncle Abe came to her house alone. It wouldn't be respectable." Hannah laughed. "And I don't think he'd go without us. He'd be afraid she'd get the wrong idea. With us along, he gets a big dinner, the kind of food he enjoys . . ."

"No chicken," Molly interrupted and Mama laughed again, and nodded.

"Plenty of attention and flattery," she said. "And no marriage talk. A perfect evening for him. No wonder he's always in a good mood there."

They were both laughing as they climbed the stairs to their room.

A few days later Molly met Cleo outside the boarding house.

"What are you doing today?" she asked.

Molly shrugged.

"Nothing much. Going to the store, so Mama can get to the Settlement House. Miss Bauman's arranging some tutoring sessions, besides the night classes, to help her write better in English. She's doing fine with reading, but writing's hard for her and she can't practice much when she's working. Until school starts, I'll fill in so she can get more tutoring during the day."

"When does she eat lunch?" Cleo said.

"At the Settlement House, while she studies. Miss Bauman's a big help and Mama says she's like that with everybody."

"I hear people in our boarding house talk about her, too. Granny has two friends Miss Bauman's teaching to read. They're from Alabama and worked from the time they were little, so they never did get to go to school."

The girls sat on the steps in front of Molly's boarding house, morning sun warm on their shoulders.

"Maybe that's what I'll do after I go to college. Work at the Settlement House, like Miss Bauman."

"I thought you wanted to be a teacher."

"She is a teacher for Mama and a lot of people, like your Granny's friends, but she does other things, too. It's called social work," Molly explained.

Cleo stretched out her long legs and tilted her head back to capture the sun's rays.

"What other things?" she said.

"Helping people get jobs. Or clothes, if they can't afford them. She found a place to stay for a man in my mother's class when his wife and baby came from Lithuania. His relatives didn't have room for all of them."

"Lithuania? Is that a country?" Cleo said.

"I think it's somewhere near Poland. Anyhow, Mama says Miss Bauman does all kinds of different, helpful things."

"I guess that'd be a good job to have. I wish I knew what I wanted to be, like you and Victor."

"You have plenty of time to decide. Maybe, when we go back to Central in a few weeks, you'll get some ideas."

"I hope. Granny says I'll probably meet a nice boy, get married, and stay home to take care of our babies, but my Daddy says I can be anything I want and he'll help me to do it."

"He's right, Cleo. You're very smart," Molly said.

Cleo sat up, looked at her friend, and shrugged.

"Maybe. I'm smart enough to know you'd better get going so your Mama can leave for the Settlement House."

Molly jumped up. "I almost forgot."

"Before you leave, Victor said to tell you his music job went so well they have two more dates lined up. He wants to celebrate with us tonight. We're supposed to meet him after supper at a place called Carbone's on Wylie Avenue. I'll wait for you here at about seven."

"Okay. Now I better go."

Slightly breathless from her rush to get to the store, Molly didn't notice much at first, except that there were no customers and her mother didn't look ready to leave. Hannah, arranging trays in the glass display case, seemed distracted. It didn't take long for Molly to learn why.

"Young lady," her uncle bellowed from the back of the store, wiping his hands on his blood-stained apron. "Are you trying to get me in trouble?"

Molly, baffled, said, "What do you mean?"

"That woman, that writer woman was back. The snooty one in the shirt that looks like it has too much starch. Cather, she said her name was."

Molly's stomach lurched. She'd forgotten about the demanding visitor who'd insisted on seeing the cellar.

The rasp of her uncle's voice seemed to bounce off the walls of the empty store.

"She came in here like she owned the place and said she had a few questions about the chicken cellar. I didn't know what she was talking about but she told me you'd shown her where I raise my hens. What was in your head, to take her downstairs? You want the health inspectors to close my business? Then where would we be? You and your mother could be back in Poland, fighting the peasants with the rest of your family."

"Please, Abe," her mother interrupted. "Molly meant no harm. She didn't understand."

"She understands everything else, so how come she couldn't say no to that busybody? Writing a story for her newspaper in Nebraska, the woman says, and she kept asking questions."

"I tried to stop her, but she pushed right past me and went downstairs." That's slightly exaggerated, Molly thought, but the lady had been insistent. "She wouldn't take no for an answer."

Her uncle shook his head grimly. "What a lot of nerve. When I wouldn't answer questions that were none of her business, she kept pestering me, so I threw her out."

Molly's eyes widened, her mouth open. "You threw the lady out! How could you do that?"

"He means he told her to leave. He didn't push her out the door," her mother said.

"From now on, Molly, when you're here, just wait on the customers and sell them what they want. Don't give anybody a tour of my business. If they're nosy troublemakers, like that Cather woman, tell them to come back when the owner's here. Understood?"

"Yes," she answered, holding back her anger. She looked at her mother, pale and quiet behind the counter. "Go to see Miss Bauman now. Everything will be all right here."

As she prepared to leave Hannah brushed past her daughter and whispered, "Do what he says. Don't make more trouble."

Uncle Abe was turning her mother into a scared, meek creature. "Don't make trouble" was what their neighbors in Swidnik said when the police came to their town. They were so afraid someone might annoy an official, say the wrong thing, and every Jewish family would suffer. More taxes, more restrictions—maybe a store mysteriously catching fire.

Molly knew it was different in America, where people didn't need to be afraid of the police. Patrolman O'Neill, the man the kids called Cap, was her uncle's friend. Sometimes he bought the little children ice cream cones. Now, instead of the police, her mother was afraid of Uncle Abe. She worried she would lose her job so they couldn't pay the rent and would be thrown out into the street. Molly couldn't live always being afraid. She had to go to school and get a good job, so she could take care of her mother.

Until Hannah returned several hours later, Molly went about her tasks exactly as her uncle directed.

FIVE

Waiting for Cleo that evening outside the boarding house, Molly thought about the woman whose probing questions had angered her uncle. She wondered if, when she was older, she could be as bold and fearless as Miss Cather. She doubted it; maybe a person had to be born in America to feel like that.

As it was, she was still afraid of so many things: appearing stupid, behaving foolishly, not knowing how to react to the strange, new things she had yet to learn about this country. Even after three years of American schooling, she feared that her classmates and teachers might not understand what she said.

Molly sighed. She knew that Uncle Abe, quick to flare up in anger, was also quick to get over it. Next time she saw him, his annoyance with her would be past, but she didn't like to upset her mother, who already had enough on her mind.

"Hey, girl, you look about a million miles away," said Cleo, coming out of her building. "What's going on inside that odd head of yours?"

Molly described what'd happened with Uncle Abe and the inquisitive visitor.

Cleo chuckled. "Wish I'd been there to see your uncle toss out Miss High and Mighty. That would've been a sight!"

"He didn't toss her, only told her to leave."

Cleo laughed harder.

"Your English's improved so much, sometimes I forget how a few words can still mix you up. The idea of your uncle picking up the lady in the starched shirt like one of his chickens and throwing her out the door is funny, but there's toss and there's toss. I have to teach you the difference."

"You really think my English is good?" Molly said.

"I wouldn't say so if I didn't. Haven't I spent these years since you came correcting your words?"

Molly smiled. "Laughing sometimes, but helping. Some of the kids in our class made fun of me, but you never did."

"Neither did Vittorio, even after he became Victor," Cleo said.

"He was making just as many mistakes so he couldn't laugh at mine!"

They walked along Wylie Avenue toward the place where they were meeting Victor. Molly liked to look at the windows of the Italian groceries where long sausages, fat balls of cheese wrapped in cord, and chains of dried red peppers and garlic hung from hooks in the ceiling. As customers opened the doors, heady, ripe aromas wafted on the warm evening air.

"It's funny about Victor," Cleo said. "His parents met in Pittsburgh after they came from Italy and got married in a church a few blocks from our boarding houses. But Victor never spoke a word of English until he started school. When I met him in the seventh grade he still had an Italian accent."

"I tried to speak English in Poland. Papa studied it—he's very smart and knows three or four languages—and wanted us all to learn, to get ready for America. He could read it fine out of his books, but had no one to help him learn how to say the words." Molly smiled. "Now I know he pronounced them more like Yiddish than English. When Mama and I came here the words sounded so odd I didn't understand them until we'd read out loud at school. Then I knew some. Everyone talked so fast I couldn't tell what they were saying. Except you, Cleo. You talked slower."

"That's because I come from down South, honeychile. We all talked slow in Alabama. Talk slow, think fast—that's my motto. Look, there's Victor waiting for us in front of Carbone's."

They walked into a large, parlor-like room, inhaling the sweet aroma. Suspended from the high ceiling, propeller fans made lazy circles, their whirr barely audible above the steady chatter in Italian that always reminded Molly of music.

Customers talked and greeted friends as they waited in line before display cases topped with black and white marble counters. Victor led them to the back, to another room where round tables were surrounded by wire-backed chairs. Molly noticed several sofas covered in dark red and purple shiny fabric. On one of them five small children, the girls in pink ruffled dresses, wriggled on the cushions.

"We're going to have Carbone's ice cream banquet. Famous throughout the city," Victor proclaimed. "You two are privileged to be in the best spumoni parlor in Pittsburgh."

"What's spumoni?" Molly said and Cleo added, "Never heard of it."

"Spumoni's like extra-rich ice cream, better than American, with nuts and different flavors. Not dull vanilla, much tastier. Sit right down here while I find Mr. Carbone and get him to fix us the ice cream banquet."

The girls sat on a sofa and surveyed the room. Families were gathered around most of the tables, talking fast, their hands waving to emphasize their ideas. On another sofa, a man and woman sat together, he singing softly and holding her hand. Molly decided this place was fun to visit even without the ice cream.

Victor returned, carrying a tray covered with desserts in thick glass dishes and three flowered plates, one for each of them. He pulled up a small table for the tray and explained its contents.

"See, this is spumoni, three different flavors in layers in one slice. Taste it, see what you think."

After grunts of approval they dug their spoons deeper to get all the flavors together.

"I told you," Victor said, looking smug while holding a spoonful of spumoni. "When we finish this, we have gelato. What flavor would you like? Chocolate? Banana? Carbone's specialty is hazelnut. You want to try it?"

Molly and Cleo were too busy eating to answer Vic's rapidly fired questions. After she'd scraped the last of the spumoni from her plate Cleo said, "I don't know what gelato is, so how can I answer?"

"Like ice cream, only much creamier and with a more—" he paused, searching for the word—"intense flavor." Then he grinned, showing straight white teeth and great self-satisfaction at his language skills.

"Intense? What a good word. Miss Bauman would approve," Molly said.

"Who's she?" Victor said.

"She works with my mother and other immigrants at the Settlement House. Her family's lived here for three generations but she learned to speak the immigrants' languages—Polish, Italian, Croatian, Yiddish—to help the newcomers. When they do well in their lessons she gives them prizes."

"What kind of prizes?" asked Cleo, licking her spoon.

"She gave Mama a handkerchief with yellow and blue flowers embroidered on it. Mama told her she'd never owned one so beautiful."

"Nobody gave me presents when I was learning English," Victor said.

"The teacher didn't throw you out when you said dumb things; that was your prize," Cleo answered, putting her empty dish on the tray. "Now, what about that gelato? I'll take hazelnut."

"Me, too." Molly said.

"I'll get some demitasse, too," Victor said as he left, carrying the tray.

"Do you know what that is?" Molly said.

"No, but if it's as good as the stuff we've had so far, I'll take my chances," Cleo answered.

Victor returned with a tray holding three bowls heaped with golden mounds studded with brown nuts. There were also miniature cups and saucers of white porcelain, the cups filled with a dark liquid sending up aromatic steam. Sugar cubes in a crystal bowl and small spoons were also on the tray.

"Those are the smallest coffee cups I ever saw," Molly said. "In my family we use mugs for coffee and glasses for tea."

"This isn't your everyday coffee. Mr. Carbone buys the beans from Italy, then roasts and grinds them himself, to make strong demitasse like people drink in Italy. Let it cool while you eat some gelato, then take small sips to see if you like it."

Molly thought the gelato, airy, cool, and so creamy it melted on her tongue, the best dessert she'd ever tasted. She took a small sip of the coffee and was surprised by its strong, bitter flavor.

Victor watched her reaction. "Too much coffee taste? My *paesanos* like it that way. When you get used to it, the kind most people drink tastes like dishwater."

"How do you know what dishwater tastes like?" Cleo said, pushing aside her cup. "And I thought that in Italy everyone drinks wine."

"Vino. They do. And nobody washes dishes. When they finish eating they throw them against the wall."

Molly considered that, frowning slightly, until she noticed her friends looking at her.

Victor said, "We have to stop teasing her because Molly believes everything we tell her."

"Not always," she answered. "Sometimes I don't understand the way Americans joke. In Poland nobody did that. You could get sent to jail."

When Cleo looked at her doubtfully, Molly laughed. "See, Cleo believes everything, too."

Cleo turned to look at the people sitting near them. "What are those folks eating?"

Victor turned to see, then said, "Torrone, teta, anise biscuits. Would you like some?"

"Thanks, but I couldn't eat another bite," Cleo said.

"And I didn't understand a thing you said," Molly added.

"Torrone is candy made of honey and nuts," Victor explained. "Teta is a spicy cookie and anise biscuits taste like licorice."

"Oh," Molly said. She had no idea what licorice meant or tasted like, but she didn't want to ask. She'd have her mother find out from Miss Bauman.

"See the little white-covered candies?" Victor said. "They're sugar-coated almonds. At weddings, guests throw them at the bride and groom."

"I'd rather throw rice," Cleo said. "You hit the bride with those things, she'll be wearing bruises along with her white dress."

Molly laughed. "You're not supposed to aim at her, unless you're the girlfriend the groom didn't marry."

Victor shook his head.

"In Poland you'd go to jail for that."

After they'd thanked Victor for the party and said good night, the girls walked slowly back to their boarding houses. It was a warm night; with no breeze blowing, the air was thick with acrid smoke from the mills. People sat on the steps leading to their doors, talking and watching children playing on the sidewalks. An old woman, not much taller than the broom she was wielding, muttered as she swept a black carpet of dust from her doorstep.

Molly and Cleo stepped around three small girls playing hopscotch. Further along, they stepped into the street to avoid interrupting some children jumping rope. The children chanted a counting rhyme in cadence with the rope's arcs.

Hunched on the stoop outside Cleo's building a man sat alone, barely nodding as they approached. A black patch covered his left eye; his left arm, the hand bent and missing two fingers, hung motionless at his side.

"He makes me shiver," Molly whispered. "Whenever I see him he just moves his head a little and never speaks."

"I think he's scary, too," Cleo said, "but Granny always says hello to him and asks how he's doing. He doesn't answer, just nods his head. Gran says we should remember our manners because every soul needs some human kindness. He got hurt in a mill accident and can't work anymore, so he sits around all the time, with no one to look after him."

"Doesn't he have a family?" Molly said.

"He did, a wife and a little boy. Granny said his wife got tired of living with him like that and left. She took their boy with her."

"No wonder he looks so sad," Molly said.

Cleo nodded. "Granny says we should be extra nice to him. Sometimes she takes him soup she made, or some ribs. We don't have spareribs that often ourselves, so it's usually soup."

Cleo slipped past the man on the stoop and went inside. She lived on the top floor and Molly usually waited until she climbed the stairs and waved from the window of what she called the front room. In it were a few chairs, a table and a sink, and the big green couch her father slept on. Unlike Molly and her mother, the Paysons did their own cooking and didn't have to eat in the boarding house dining room.

Molly knew her mother would've preferred that, too, but they couldn't afford an apartment, as the Paysons' rooms were called, but only a bedroom, with the use of the dining room for their meals. Sometimes, when they ate at Uncle Abe's, Mama would cook, preparing the kinds of foods they'd eaten in their old home. She and her mother both tired of the watery soups and fatty meats Mrs. Levin served at the boarding house, but they understood that, with the low rents she received from her boarders, she couldn't, as she often said, afford to serve banquets.

When Cleo had waved from her upstairs window Molly went into her adjoining building and up the stairs to the third floor. She grinned, remembering the ice cream banquet. Wouldn't that make Mrs. Levin's eyes pop? She might even pause in darning the endless basket of socks waiting in her lap.

SIX

Hannah Klein looked up from the book she was studying, her frown replaced by a smile for her daughter.

"To spell these words, when they don't sound like their letters, is impossible. Whoever thought up English didn't like us greenhorns—and greenhorn is a silly thing to call a newcomer to this country. Just when I think I know something, along comes another puzzle."

"Americans trying to learn Polish or Yiddish would say the same and you know both. You're too hard on yourself, Mama."

Hannah sighed and closed her book. "Miss Bauman says so, too, but I want to know enough to teach your brothers and help Papa when they come. The boys probably aren't practicing much."

"Maybe Papa should tell them to write to us in English," Molly said.

"A good idea. I'll say so in my next letter. But you know how lazy your brothers are about writing, especially Simon, and Papa's too busy to push them. It's hard for him, too, with no one around who knows enough English to practice speaking. Without the Settlement House I wouldn't know much, either."

"They'll learn fast when they get here; my brothers will go to school, like I do."

"You're a better student, Molly. I wouldn't tell them that, it would hurt their feelings. They need to earn a living, so I hope they learn a trade here or have a business, like Uncle Abe."

"I'm going to earn my own living, too. In this country girls can be independent and I'll be a teacher or a social worker like Miss Bauman. That's why I need to go to college."

"I can't think about that now. When your father comes and we're a real family again, we'll figure what to do. Now, please, help me practice these words."

The last, hot days of summer quickly passed. When Molly wasn't helping in her uncle's store or assisting her mother with language lessons she explored the neighborhood with Cleo. Victor joined them when he could, but he had less time; his father and uncles insisted he go along on their masonry jobs. He needed, they told him, to learn their trade.

"I don't like to go," he told the girls as they walked together along Logan Street. "The more they show me how to lay stones, the more they talk about how I should get a job soon. 'You a big guy now,' Uncle Luigi says, 'When I was your age I was workin' road crews, bringin' home money.'"

Vic stopped to move a wooden barrel heaped with green cabbages back against a storefront, making more room on the crowded sidewalk. The pungent cabbage smell mixed with the odors of cheese and garlic. Scraps of old newspapers drifted in spirals of coal dust each time a hot wind blew.

Molly noticed the bulging muscles in Victor's arms as he pushed against the weight of the barrel. When she'd met him he was thin, scrawny. Now he looked like an athlete, husky and strong from his work lifting and shaping bulky stones. She understood why his uncle believed he was ready to take on a man's job.

"I can't argue with Luigi or my father," Victor said as they continued walking. "They don't understand my wanting to be a mathematician. They've always worked with their hands so they're suspicious of formulas on paper. 'Scribbles', my uncle calls them." He smiled, but Molly noticed that his eyes were somber.

"How about your uncle the violinist?" Cleo said. "He must understand."

"He does, but he says I have to put the math aside because my family's depending on me to help out. They want to move away from the Hill, buy a house in East Liberty. Mama talks about it all the time."

"You can't do that," Cleo said, her voice rising. "We'd miss you. You have to stay in the neighborhood with us."

Victor laughed. "It's not like I'm going to Naples. We'd still see each other."

"Not at school everyday," Molly said.

They were silent as the three of them considered that possibility.

Then Victor spoke, trying to sound more reassuring than Molly believed he felt. "Maybe it's all talk and won't happen."

As they passed a clock in a store window, he said, "I didn't know it was so late. I have to go practice for another wedding where we're supposed to play."

As he hurried off, Cleo said, "Wouldn't it be fun if we could go to that wedding and hear Victor play? We could dance and have a great old time."

"Sure. The bride's family would be happy to have two strangers come to eat their food and join the dancing," Molly answered.

"Who would notice? We'd blend right into the crowd, especially me."

With that, they both laughed so loudly people on the sidewalk turned to stare disapprovingly at the rowdy girls.

Two days before school was to start Cleo came into the poultry store. Molly was sweeping the floor while her mother worked behind the counter.

"Morning, Mrs. Klein. How are you today, ma'am?"

Hannah smiled at her daughter's friend and returned her greeting. She thought Cleo the best-mannered young person she'd ever met. At first, Hannah worried that Molly would be lonely in a city full of strangers and confusing experiences, but she'd readily adjusted to her new world. Cleo and that nice Italian boy were good friends to her.

Hannah had made a few friends, too, at the Settlement House. The women in her classes talked about their families and their reactions to strange new customs in America, but she didn't have much to say in return. Except for Molly, her family was still in the old country. Abe was her husband's uncle, but often seemed more like an employer than family. She didn't tell him and certainly not her acquaintances how much she missed her husband and sons.

At times, Hannah's longing for them was a great ache in her heart that made her want to cry out in pain. She needed so much to have someone to talk to, really talk, the way she and Nathan used to after the children were asleep. They would share the events of the day, her husband relating his customers' stories and she describing the children's experiences and their neighbors' gossip. Often nothing important, but if she was troubled Nathan would listen and make her feel better. Now, she tried to avoid sharing her worries with Molly—after all, she was the mother and supposed to be in control—and, besides, Molly was busy building her new life here.

Her daughter, Hannah knew, had made a better, faster adjustment to America than she. When she'd said that to Miss Bauman during one of their tutoring sessions, the older woman didn't seem surprised.

"Of course. She's young, she's learned English more quickly because of school and talking with her friends. It's harder for you; your uncle and most of your customers speak to you in Polish or Yiddish. You should be proud of Molly's progress in becoming an American."

"Yes . . ." Hannah had hesitated. She wasn't sure how to say what she felt or whether she should say anything at all. Miss Bauman might think she didn't appreciate the help she was getting at the Settlement House.

The director had looked at her, her gaze shrewd and penetrating. "But you're a little troubled by it? Are you afraid Molly's forgetting the life she had before you came here and her family back in Poland? Maybe you think she's becoming a little too American, but you feel guilty saying that?"

Hannah had nodded, eyes filling with tears. Miss Bauman saw into her soul. Although she was anxious about her mentor's reaction she was relieved, too, that her unspoken fears could be shared at last.

Miss Bauman had leaned toward her student and taken her hand. "Feeling that way's nothing to be ashamed of. Molly isn't being selfish, only making a healthy adjustment to her new country. She still loves her father and brothers. It's natural for her to be caught up in her new life just as it's natural for you to yearn for your family and the past when you were together. You're doing what you can to help, with your letters and the money you try to save to bring them here. Keep it up, and be proud of your daughter's progress."

Then she'd turned back to the newspaper before them. "Now, back to work. Read this article for me, slowly, taking care to pronounce the words properly."

Hannah told herself that Miss Bauman was right about Molly but sometimes, in the quiet before sleep, when the longing for her husband and sons made her whole body ache, Hannah wasn't so sure. She remembered an earlier conversation when her daughter had returned from the store.

"Mrs. Ansheloff came in to buy some eggs this afternoon, Mama. She asked about you."

"She's a kind lady. Did she say how her husband is feeling? He was too sick to work last week."

"I didn't really talk to her," Molly had answered. "I can't understand what she says most of the time, even when she thinks she's speaking English. It gets all mixed up with Russian and she waves her hands around, trying to explain."

Molly had ducked her head. "I know it's not nice, but sometimes I can hardly keep from laughing, her English sounds so peculiar. It's a good thing Uncle Abe knows what she's saying."

"Is that what you think of me, too?" Hannah hadn't been able to keep the sadness from her voice. "I sound funny, maybe make you ashamed of me? Another greenhorn, like Sophie Ansheloff?"

Her daughter had hugged and reassured her and Hannah reminded herself of how much her daughter loved her family. When the others came from Poland Molly would help them, not be embarrassed because they were different.

These disturbing thoughts faded as laughter from Molly and Cleo brought Hannah back to the present. "You were a big help this morning, Molly. Abe'll be back soon, so you can go with Cleo now."

Outside, the girls walked past women shopping for food and merchants arranging wooden crates jammed with fruit so ripe that bees hovered over them. A barrel filled with fat pickles floating in brine made Cleo wrinkle her nose.

"Too much to smell on a hot morning."

"You wouldn't complain if they were doughnuts," Molly said.

"Come to my place and see the clothes Granny made for me for school," Cleo suggested, and Molly nodded.

They passed a dry goods store and stopped to look in the window. Bolts of fabrics were draped to display their patterns and stripes.

"I'm glad my grandmother didn't buy any of that. I don't want to start school looking like a flower garden," Cleo said.

"What about those red and blue stripes? You'd be mistaken for a barber's pole," Molly said.

Molly was pleased with her joke. There'd been a time when she didn't know that barbers advertised their trade by displaying striped poles, or that carved wooden Indians signaled that cigars were sold inside the store. In her Polish town there were no such things; mothers or fathers trimmed the children's hair and not very often at that. When they'd arrived in Pittsburgh Molly insisted that her long braids be cut off and her hair worn short, like most of the girls in her class. Her mother reluctantly agreed and they'd paid a rare visit to Mr. Barnes, the neighborhood barber.

When Cleo opened the door to her apartment Mrs. Payson was sitting near the window, pale green cotton cloth folded beside her. Covered with blue pillows and a matching quilt, the place where she sat was so artfully disguised as a sofa, visitors wouldn't know it was a bed. She and her grandmother slept in a bigger bed in the adjoining room, which also had a desk for Cleo, a chest of drawers, and a sewing machine. In this room, which Cleo called the parlor, there were the sofa where her father slept, a rocking chair, a table and three chairs, a stove, sink, icebox and, squeezed into the remaining space, Mr. Payson's piano.

Molly sat on the bench next to the piano. She liked to touch the keys, cool even on sweltering summer days. Although the piano was old—the wood was scratched and a chunk missing from one corner—it was polished to a deep, ebony glow. Stacks of sheet music were arranged on its boxy top.

Cleo's grandmother smiled at her. "Honey, you choose that bench whenever you come here. And I notice you always touch the keys. Do you play piano?"

"No, but I like the way the keys feel and the shiny wood," Molly said.

Mrs. Payson was a tall, stately woman with gray hair that curled close to her head and fine lines around her eyes that deepened when she laughed. Molly liked her laughter, which seemed to start at her toes and fill her body with a deep, rich echo that made Molly want to laugh, too.

"I do declare that's as good a reason as any for wanting to sit there. Lots of people have taken to that bench, beginning with Cleo's gran'daddy. Her own father hired a truck, using every penny he'd saved, to haul it here from Alabama. He said it was worth it and I believe it every time he sits down to play."

"I heard him once when I came to see Cleo. He played for a little while before he had to leave for his shift at the hotel. It was beautiful, with sounds that tickled my ears and made me want to dance. I never heard anything like it before."

"Guess there's not much demand for ragtime in Poland," Cleo said and her grandmother laughed that deep, happy growl that made Molly join her.

"How would you know what they play, you sassy girl?" Mrs. Payson said, shaking her head at Cleo.

"Molly's told me a lot, just like I tell her about us and the club where Daddy plays when he doesn't have to work. Couldn't Molly come with us sometime to hear him?"

Mrs. Payson looked thoughtful. "I don't know about that, Cleo. She might feel kinda' strange, being there."

"I'd like to," Molly said. "If it's all right with Mr. Payson."

"He'd be pleased you want to hear him," Cleo's grandmother said. She paused, choosing her next words carefully. "Only, everyone at the club's colored and you might feel funny, being different."

Molly said, "Since I came to America I nearly always feel dif-ferent. Unless you think the other people would mind."

"I'll talk to William and see what he thinks. What with his new job, I don't know how often he'll be playing at the club. But now, Cleo, I want you to try on this shirtwaist and see if the sleeves are right. The way you're growing they may be too short since I measured your arms three whole days ago."

"Grandmother, how you do ex-ag-ger-ate." They all laughed at the way she stretched out the last word.

"Does your father have a new job?" Molly said.

"Didn't I tell you the big news? He's starting at the steel mill next week. He'll have to work different shifts all the time and it's much harder than the hotel, but he's happy because the pay's good and he's wanted to get in at the mill ever since we moved here." She smiled. "You should've seen him when he found out. He was dancing around this room, then making up songs on the piano about how rich we're going to be."

Mrs. Payson said, "I haven't seen so much excitement around here since the President came to town and waved at us."

Molly's eyes widened. "The President? The President of the United States came here?"

"He wasn't in our parlor, if that's what you think," Cleo said. "We lined up along the street with everybody else to see him. He was riding in a big, black carriage and he took off his hat and waved it in our direction. Granny was sure he was saying hello to us."

"I can't believe it," Molly said. "The United States President passing right by you! That could never happen in Swidnik."

"Course not, silly," Cleo said. "What would the President be doing in Swidnik?"

Molly ignored her. "When was that?" she asked Mrs. Payson.

"A few years ago. I think it was the winter of 1897. President McKinley and his wife came in a special train to Union Station. Guns on the bluff above the river fired an official salute the morning they arrived. The noise was so loud I was afraid this old building would tumble down."

"Weren't you here then, Molly?" Cleo said.

"We came from Poland that summer. I guess we didn't understand what was happening. Uncle Abe probably knew, but I don't remember hearing about it."

"It was something! The streetcars stopped running and the downtown stores were empty, Daddy said. He left the hotel to be with us for the parade. That was the biggest celebration I ever did see."

Granny laughed. "Cleo was cheering the soldiers and they just kept coming, marching in step up and down the hills. It was a grand sight."

"Tell Molly about the party for the President's wife," Cleo said.

Molly stared. "Did you go, Mrs. Payson? Did you talk to Mrs. McKinley?"

Cleo's grandmother threw back her head and laughed until her eyes teared. She wiped at them with her handkerchief.

"Lordy, child, I don't know about the old country, but around here colored folks don't go to lunch with high society! One of the ladies I clean for was invited to the party. Her friend is Mrs. Pitcairn, the wife of the superintendent of the Pennsylvania Railroad, and she was the hostess. The lady I work for is an outright snob; she loves to brag about the high class folks she knows. She ran out of acquaintances to tell who was there, what they wore, and what Mrs. McKinley said so she started following me as I worked, describing the details."

Mrs. Payson shook her head. "When she finished with me, she told Celia, who does the laundry; Max, the grocery delivery man; even little Georgie, who brings the newspaper every day. She kept Max so long, repeating everything, his boss threatened to fire him for loafing on the job."

"Tell Molly what the lady said, Granny," Cleo said, making an exasperated face at her friend.

"It was the most elegant luncheon she'd ever attended. She used that word 'elegant' over and over. The house was filled with flowers sent all the way from New York. The food was prepared by fancy cooks—chefs, she called them—from Sherry's of New York, whatever that is. In the parlor, great big vases were filled with pink chrysanthemums named Pitcairn, after the hostess."

"That's the part I like best," Cleo said. "When I'm famous, I'd like a rose named after me. The red Cleopatra."

"More likely a weed, the wild way you're growing," her grandmother said.

"What else did she say about the party?" Molly persisted.

"I swear, you're as bad as Cleo. That child didn't give me a minute's peace till she heard every detail." Mrs. Payson sighed and continued. "Around the dining room urns were filled with palms and ferns and on the tables there were bouquets of American Beauty roses. The stairway to the second floor was lined with white and gold chrysanthemums in clusters so thick only two people could walk together on the twelve-foot wide stairs."

"Twelve feet! That's wider than this room," Molly said.

"You could take away the posies and put our whole apartment on those stairs, honey," Mrs. Payson said, laughing.

"Tell about the way the President's wife entered," Cleo said.

"Very grand, my lady said. Elegant. She does like that word! Musicians played a waltz and all the guests waited at the bottom of the stairs. Down came Mrs. McKinley holding Mrs. Pitcairn's arm, with all those chrysanthemums around them and sunlight coming through the stained glass windows shining on them like rainbow halos. People applauded like they were at a show."

"What did they eat?" Molly said.

"She didn't get around to that. She decided I was wasting too much time and told me to get back to cleaning the kitchen," Mrs. Payson said.

"But she was talking to you," Molly said.

Mrs. Payson's face turned serious. "Don't matter none. In her mind, I was the lazy one wasting her good money. That's the way it is, Molly. She probably complained to her friends." Then she brightened. "We were talking before about how happy Cleo's daddy is about his new job."

Molly nodded.

"With the extra money, William says I might be able to quit one of my cleaning jobs for time to sew and do some dressmaking."

"Maybe you could work in one of those dress shops downtown, Granny, where the society ladies shop," Cleo said.

"I doubt it. Those places aren't ready for colored help. That's all right. I can sew right here, for folks in the neighborhood."

"My mother thinks you do beautiful work, Mrs. Payson. She always tells me how pretty Cleo's dresses are."

"Your mama's a nice lady. I like to talk with her when I buy your uncle's chicken."

"I wish she didn't work there," Molly said, glad to say the words to someone who'd understand. "She's not very strong—that's one reason Papa sent her here, to feel healthier. But she gets so tired standing behind the counter all day. She doesn't complain, only says we should be grateful to Uncle Abe for helping us. All she wants is my father and brothers to be here, too."

"That's what she told me," Cleo's grandmother said. "I said she has to have faith, keep praying and believing it will happen."

"If only she was happier," Molly said.

Cleo saw the hint of tears glistening in her friend's dark eyes.

"Let's look at the clothes Granny made me. There's a surprise for you."

"For me?" Molly followed Cleo into the bedroom.

Soon, Mrs. Payson heard Molly's voice rising in delight. Molly came out beaming, wearing a blue blouse, its high collar trimmed with white lace.

"It's beautiful and it fits exactly right. Thank you so much," she said, hugging Cleo's grandmother.

"You're welcome, sugar. It's a present to celebrate the new school year. I know you and Cleo are going to do fine. And so's your mother, Molly, so don't be worrying that pretty little head."

Molly nodded, thanked her again, and rejoined Cleo to admire her new wardrobe.

SEVEN

The next morning, wearing her new blouse, Molly prepared for classes at Central High School.

Hannah Klein studied her daughter. "The blouse is so pretty. Mrs. Payson should be a dressmaker."

Molly hurried out to meet Cleo and they walked toward Central, an imposing stone structure on a bluff overlooking the train station. In the gray fog of early morning the building dominated the landscape, its walls darkened and grimy from an accretion of soot drifting up from the steel mills in the valley. Somber and bleak as the school appeared, Molly reveled in going, reminding herself that she was a registered, official student.

In Swidnik there was no high school; a few young people from the village were admitted to a secondary school ten miles away, if their parents could pay the tuition. Simon spent hours traveling each way. There was little money left for David's tuition. For her, a girl, there was none at all. She would not have been able to go to high school if she'd stayed in Poland. When others complained about their long days in the dark, ugly building, she wanted to tell them they were lucky.

She didn't, of course. Timid still, Molly feared being laughed at or ridiculed. She was self-conscious about her accent, although Cleo and Victor both told her it wasn't at all noticeable.

"It's practically gone," Victor had said when they'd met last week. "You sound almost as good as I do."

"But without the Italian accent," Cleo added, ignoring the face Victor made.

Molly was trying to decide if she wanted to be a teacher or a social worker like Miss Bauman. She would study her teachers closely this year. What she saw would help make up her mind.

"It's time for English class," Cleo reminded her after they'd been assigned a homeroom. "I hear our new teacher is pretty strict."

"What's her name?" asked Victor, walking along the corridor with them.

"Mary Beth didn't say, only that she expects a lot from her students."

"We'll know soon enough," Molly said as they took seats and waited.

The door opened and in strode a young woman wearing a white shirtwaist with stiffly starched collar and black tie that matched her skirt. Her hair was brushed back from a low forehead. She placed a stack of books on her desk and turned to face the class, her eyes, an unusual gray-blue, studying them.

Molly covered her mouth with her hand to suppress a groan. The teacher observed her briefly, then spoke. "My name is Cather; it rhymes with rather. We shall be studying literature together and working hard on writing and language skills. You may notice that my speech patterns sound a bit different from yours. That's because I grew up in Nebraska, in a town much smaller than Pittsburgh. Where I lived, there are no steel mills, only farms and small businesses. Another difference is that in Nebraska the sky is usually a bright blue and the air smells sweet and fresh. However, we must adjust to our circumstances; that's an important life lesson."

Watching her straight stance and the way she looked at the students as if she could see directly into their heads, just as she'd behaved in the store, Molly knew she wouldn't want to argue with Willa Cather, no matter what Uncle Abe said.

"Be aware that I expect a great deal of effort and diligence from my students. You'll have many writing assignments to complete. They're especially important to me because I'm a writer as well as your teacher. I studied at the University of Nebraska, then came here to work for a magazine. I still send articles to newspapers in my home state and work at creating short stories and poetry. I persevere, striving to write well; you'll do the same. Are there any questions?"

Her inquiry was met with silence as the students assessed this unusual woman, so different from the other, older faculty members. She had a low, pleasant voice, but her manner was brisk and direct as she paced before them, calling the roll and asking for repetitions to get the pronunciations right. She called the boys by their last names and used "Miss" for the girls.

Molly kept her head down. Her English teacher for the entire year would be the relentless investigator of the chicken cellar, who'd gotten her into trouble with her uncle. Squirming in her seat, she also remembered that Miss Cather returned to the store and so annoyed Uncle Abe that he'd thrown her out. This was the woman she'd see everyday! She could only hope the teacher wouldn't remember her.

Cleo, behind Molly, nudged her and she looked up. Miss Cather was beside her.

"And your name, young lady?" she said.

Molly cleared her throat several times before the words came out, as the teacher watched, eyes boring into her.

"Thank you, Miss Klein. And how is the poultry business?"

Molly's heart thumped. She swallowed. "Fine," came out in an odd squeak. She could feel Cleo staring at her back.

The teacher nodded and moved on to the next student, making notes in a small tablet. Molly dreaded to think what was written about her. Or, maybe, she'd drawn a chicken next to her name!

Back at her desk Miss Cather placed her notebook and pen on the tidy surface of her desk. She picked up the chalk and wrote, "A Summer Stroll" on the blackboard, then turned back to the class, eyes bright.

"I believe the ability to write clearly and effectively will determine your success in your future endeavors. In this class, not only will you study great literature, you will write regularly, taking care to choose words that are apt and precisely describe what you wish to say. Both your minds and your imaginations must be exercised. On the board is the subject of today's essay. Choose a place where you've walked this summer and think of what you saw and experienced during that stroll. Don't be afraid to be creative."

She looked around the room; her gaze settled on her desk and a vase containing a white chrysanthemum. "If I were to describe the surface of this desk I could say that a glass tube held a flower that looked like a mound of coleslaw."

Molly was baffled by her classmates' laughter. She had no idea what the teacher meant or why it was funny. She felt Miss Cather's eyes on her and was surprised by their flash of sympathy.

"I realize that, because I come from another part of the country, I sometimes use terms unfamiliar to students here. In Nebraska, where we raise even more cabbages than cows, farmers' wives spend lots of time chopping them into bits— the cabbages, not the cows—and serving them as coleslaw. I detest the stuff myself."

More laughter. Molly joined in, grateful Miss Cather had explained without singling her out as foreign and stupid.

"Now, class, you have fifteen minutes to write about a summer stroll. Take out your notebooks and begin."

Molly soon looked forward to Miss Cather's class as the best part of the school day. She liked the literature assignments, especially long story poems like *The Rime of the Ancient Mariner*, and romantic tales about knights and their ladies. She enjoyed her teacher's breezy manner and enthusiasm when she helped them to write about what they observed, choosing the best words to describe what they meant to say.

Molly tried to explain her teacher's technique to her mother one evening. "Remember when I told you I'd like to be either a teacher or a social worker like Miss Bauman? If I decide to be a teacher, I'd want to be like Miss Cather. She's interested in each of us and, sometimes, to help us improve our writing, she tells us about her own experiences and how hard it can be to find the right words to say what she means."

Hannah Klein's smile reminded Molly of how pretty she was when her face wasn't touched by sadness.

"Miss Cather would lose patience with me. Almost four years in America and I still struggle every day to use the right English words."

Molly shook her head. "She knows about greenhorns. She told us once that when she was growing up in Red Cloud—that's far away, in a place called Nebraska—her favorite neighbors were immigrants who taught her many things."

"They were from Poland?" her mother said, surprised.

"No, from Norway and Germany. A man from Germany taught her about opera, and she loves it now."

Mrs. Klein frowned. "I don't know what that is."

"We didn't either, except for Victor. He said in Italy everyone knows opera and people go around singing it, even if they have terrible voices. That made Miss Cather laugh and she asked Victor if he'd demonstrate."

Molly's mother frowned again. "What does that mean?"

"To show, by singing himself. He declined—that means he wouldn't do it."

"You know so much, Molly. You become more American every day. Papa and your brothers won't know you when they come."

Molly's good mood faltered. She braced herself for what was coming, her mother's anxieties about their family. Instead, Hannah sounded cheerful.

"I didn't tell you, but I have been saving good news for you. In the letter that came today, Papa said he might have found someone to take over the store. Mr. Levitan—you remember him, the shoemaker? His daughter's getting married and the son-in-law, who comes from another town, wants to settle in Swidnik and is interested in our shop. If he buys the business, Papa and your brothers will apply the same day to come here."

Molly threw her arms around her mother. "Wonderful! Why didn't you tell me sooner?"

"Uncle Abe says we shouldn't get too excited, things could go wrong. Wait and see, he says, and do not expect too much."

"What a wet blanket," Molly said, investing the new phrase with all the disdain she felt Uncle Abe deserved.

Hannah looked bewildered. "Abe is a blanket?"

Molly explained about slang expressions, but her mother still looked confused.

"It's like Miss Cather telling us she comes from cowboy country. Cleo and I laughed to picture her, dressed in boots and a big hat with a brim, reciting poetry, then slapping her horse and saying giddy up."

Hannah shook her head and joined in her daughter's laughter.

Occupied with school and chores at the poultry store, Molly noticed the passage of time through the changes in her neighborhood. Leaves on the maple tree beside the boarding house turned from dusty green to a vivid scarlet that brightened the gray mornings when she left for school. When she returned the breeze hinted at winter, but the tree glowed with its own light.

Dusk arrived early. Winds thick with smoke from the mills carried the smell of coal fires, burning in most homes now to ward off the nighttime chill. At her boarding house Molly stopped to warm her hands at the big stove in the downstairs sitting room. Boarders clustered near it, reading newspapers in several languages, smoking cigarettes or cigars, and discussing the day's events.

Sitting among them was Mrs. Levin, the landlady, dressed as always in black, down to the slippers with torn seams where her black-clad toes peeked through. She said little as she darned an endless supply of mismatched socks, ignoring her own tattered footwear. Molly imagined that the boxes stacked in the hallway for shipment to European relatives were full of socks covered with tiny stitches in the heels and toes.

In the morning she and Cleo walked to Central, expecting to meet Victor along the way. But, for the last three days, he hadn't been in class.

"Do you think he's sick?" Molly asked, turning up her collar against a sharp wind. "Maybe we should go to his house."

Cleo shook her head. "You know Victor. He's strong as an ox. Something else's keeping him away. He wouldn't want to miss math and that special project he always talks about."

It's not like Cleo to worry, Molly thought. "After school, let's go find out," Molly said and Cleo nodded agreement.

Cleo wasn't the only one who was uneasy. After math class Mr. Brownell stopped them. "Have you seen Victor?" he asked. Furrowed lines creased his forehead, beneath thinning gray hair. "He was so involved in the trigonometry we've been working on he was staying after school. I don't understand his absences—unless he's sick . . ."

Mr. Brownell sounded as doubtful as Cleo.

"Molly and I are wondering the same thing," Cleo answered. "We're going to his house after school."

"Good. Please let me now what you find out. And if there's anything I can do."

The girls remembered that later, when they waited at the door to the house where Vic lived with his parents, his musician uncle, and three younger sisters.

They knocked a long time.

Mrs. Morelli, a stout, sweet-faced woman with braided black hair anchored with tortoise shell combs, smiled at them when she answered the door. Her long dark skirt and gray blouse, sleeves rolled up to her elbows, were covered with an apron from which she dusted clouds of flour.

"Not here." She gestured with rolling pin motions to show she'd been baking. The girls had first met her when she was shopping for groceries on Logan Street, with Victor along to carry the packages. She had greeted them in Italian, with her son translating the only language spoken at his home.

"Mama loves to talk. In Italian she never stops."

His mother chuckled, wagging her finger at him.

"She understands everything in English, but refuses to speak it. A stubborn lady."

Mrs. Morelli had shaken her head, but it was easy to see she didn't mind Victor's teasing.

Now, she wiped her hands against her apron, releasing puffs of flour, and extended them to the girls. "Wanta come in?"

Molly said, "We're looking for Victor. Is he sick?"

Mrs. Morelli frowned, considering the question. She shook her head. "Vittorio no sick. Go work."

Cleo and Molly exchanged glances, not sure Mrs. Morelli had understood.

"He wasn't in school this week," Cleo said, speaking slowly. "We wondered if he's all right."

"No go school. Go work with papa and uncles."

Cleo persisted. "When will he come back to school?"

Mrs. Morelli shook her head vigorously, as if to underline her words. "No school no more. Vittorio work."

The girls stared, trying to absorb what she'd said.

Mrs. Morelli added, "I tell Vittorio you come." Then she closed the door.

Silent, they walked toward their street. Cleo kicked an empty fruit crate left near the curb and sent it flying. "He told us it could happen," she said, "but I never thought he'd really do it."

Molly choked back the lump in her throat. "He can't quit. He's the best math student at Central. And you know how he talks about going to college." She turned to her friend. "Isn't it against American law, not to go to school?"

"He's old enough, so it's not illegal. It's just plain wrong."

"We'll tell Mr. Brownell tomorrow. Maybe he can do something," Molly said.

She tried to concentrate on her homework that night, working at the table while her mother rested on the bed, reading one of the books Miss Bauman helped her to borrow from the Settlement House library. They both were surprised by the knock at their door.

It was Mrs. Levin. "You have a visitor, Molly, a young man. He's waiting downstairs."

"Did he tell you his name?"

"I didn't ask. Are you coming?"

As Mrs. Levin left, sighing her displeasure at having to climb the stairs, Molly combed her hair, tucked her blouse into the waistband of her skirt, and hurried down.

Victor stood waiting, his face pale in the dim light. He twisted the cap he held in his hands.

"Victor! I'm so glad to see you. We missed you at school and Cleo and I worried you were sick."

"I'm sorry for that. I heard you came to the house." He paused, searching for words. "I guess I should've come to see you and Cleo before . . ." He looked down, avoiding her gaze. "Before I started working."

"What do you mean? You've always worked after school and summers."

Victor looked around the shadowy sitting room. Three men on a couch talked in low tones. Nearby, Mrs. Levin sat darning a sock. "Could we go for a walk?"

"I'll go upstairs and get my coat."

She and Victor moved slowly along Fulton Street. Molly hardly noticed their surroundings, she was so troubled by her friend's mood. Words, jokes, ideas, and laughter usually poured out, but now he was solemn.

"What's going on? Your mother said you were working when you should be in school."

He stared straight ahead, not looking at her. "No more school. I'm an apprentice mason now. Someday, the stones you walk on will be the handiwork of Victor Morelli." The attempt at light-heartedness came out as self-mockery.

Molly stopped and turned to him. "What about your plans? You are going to be a mathematician."

For the first time his gaze met hers and she saw the sadness in his eyes.

"Papa and my uncles say it's time to be a man, learn a man's trade. Help the family. Papa wants to move away from the Hill and buy a house. It takes money and I'm big enough and strong enough to earn some."

Molly's anger was clear in her voice. "Do they know you can earn more, lots more, if you get an education? Don't they want you to be happy?"

Victor took her arm to urge her forward. They started walking again. When he spoke his voice was flat. "My family needs the money now. To become a mathematician takes years, too long for them to wait. Maybe it would never happen. They can't afford my daydreams."

"You shouldn't give up, Victor, you mustn't. Cleo and I'll tell Mr. Brownell. He can talk to your father, explain how smart you are, and how important it is for you to study math."

"No!" Victor's shout made passersby stare. "Listen to me so you'll understand. I'm doing what needs to be done. It would shame my family for Mr. Brownell or anyone else to say such things to them. I have to take responsibility, I'm not a kid any longer."

He looked at Molly and his voice softened. "You're my friend and you want to help, but I'll be all right. I always knew being a mathematician was a dream, make-believe. Math's like that for me—a game, puzzles that are fun to solve. It can't put bread on our table or buy a house where my uncle won't have to sleep on the couch. If anybody asks, say I've decided to quit school and I'm the legal age to do that. Please, Molly, don't make me feel worse about what I'm doing. And don't let anyone shame my family."

She only nodded. Certain his decision was wrong, a waste of his talent, she understood that he could do nothing else and that, if she and Cleo tried to interfere, they'd only add to his pain.

Silently, they walked back to her boarding house. As she turned to go in, Victor took her hand. "Do you think you and Cleo can still be my friends, even if we don't see each other at school every day? Maybe get together on weekends, like when we went to Schenley Park?"

"Or had our ice cream feast?" She smiled at him. "You can count on it. No puzzle for you to solve there. How should we contact you?"

"Leave a note with my mother. She likes you two, she might even invite you for some pasta."

Molly couldn't smile, although she knew that was what Victor wanted. She waved goodbye and went inside.

Hannah shook her head when Molly told her about Victor.

"What a shame, a smart boy like that. But don't blame his family; they're trying to make a better life for him, too."

"If that's what they think, they are so wrong," Molly said, her voice loud enough that her mother reminded her of the thin walls and that the Brodskys next door needed their rest.

"There has to be a way to fix this," she said in a lower voice. "But Victor told me I can't say anything that would shame his family."

Her mother nodded. "Because people are poor doesn't mean they're not proud," Hannah said. "Miss Bauman talked at the Settlement House about pride. She says it will help us do well in America."

"It won't do Victor much good when he's in the streets chipping stones instead of learning math."

Hannah frowned. "You should not—oh, what is the word?—ah, criticize—criticize Miss Bauman. She knows what she's talking about."

Molly glared back. "Then ask Miss Bauman how pride will help Victor when his family's making him quit school and waste his brain." Molly slammed her book shut on the table and began to prepare for bed.

"Maybe I will," Hannah said. "I would not be surprised if she has an answer."

"I would. When do you see her again?"

"Tomorrow afternoon. Please come to the store right after school."

Molly nodded, hung up her clothes, and started down the hall to the bathroom.

"Try not to stay too long," her mother said. "Mrs. Brodsky complained yesterday you spend too much time in the bathroom. She says to buy a mirror for our room so you can look at yourself here and not keep the others from getting ready for work."

"Mrs. Brodsky is a nosy grouch who minds everybody's business." Molly's voice had risen again. "And I don't care if she does hear me."

EIGHT

Molly told Cleo about Victor the next morning. When her friend started to protest Molly interrupted, "It's no use. I've already said everything to him."

"I can't believe Mr. Brownell will let this happen. He's always praising Victor. The whole school's heard about his math talent."

"It doesn't matter," Molly said. "Victor doesn't want us to say anything except that he's decided to leave school. You should've seen the way he looked when he talked about shaming his family. So we can't go to Mr. Brownell for help."

Although it was late October the morning felt warm, like the return of summer. Cleo took off her coat. "I guess they'll have to close the windows at school again," she said.

On certain warm days the wind blew from the southwest and clouds of black smoke from the chimneys of the Herron Hill pumping station drifted towards their school. Students near the windows would rush to close them. Better to endure the hot, stale closeness of the rooms than be plagued with coughing seizures, watery eyes, and raw throats from inhaling the bitter fumes.

Miss Cather was late that day. "Sorry, everyone," she said, bustling in with her usual energy. Molly looked forward to seeing what she'd wear each day. It was nearly always a starched blouse and tailored skirt, but she liked colors, too. Molly paid particular attention to her ties because they were usually brightly colored. Cleo's favorite, she told Molly, was the green one, but her own choice was yellow like the flowers that bloomed in Schenley Park.

"I was checking on some information about pseudonyms or pen names like the one Mr. Samuel Clemens chose. And what would that be? Molly Klein?"

Molly was glad she'd done the assignment. She hated the embarrassment of not knowing an answer.

"Mark Twain, Miss Cather."

"Good. Who can explain why he chose that pen name?"

Cleo raised her hand. "He was a Mississippi River boat pilot and mark twain was a term pilots used for the depth of the water."

"Excellent. Names and nicknames are fascinating, don't you think? I, for example, was named for a relative called William and sometimes my friends called me Bill. When I was very young my family moved to Red Cloud, as I've told you. Such a pretty name, I thought, but my first impressions were of a place as bleak and bare as a piece of sheet iron.

"Names can be deceptive and intriguing. Think of your own classmates. Cleo Payson's name is lovely, but I suspect Cleo is a nickname. Is that correct?"

"Not exactly, ma'am. It's short for my real name, Cleopatra."

Molly heard a few snickers from the back of the room. Miss Cather scowled at two boys in the last row. "Cleopatra was a beautiful and powerful queen. Does that strike you as amusing, Holmes and Foreman?"

"No, ma'am," each answered, chastened.

Miss Cather glared again, then continued. "Thanks to Miss Payson we know why Samuel Clemens chose a river pilot's term for his *nom de plume*. Suppose we ask her now about the origin of her name."

Cleo smiled. Molly knew what was coming.

"My daddy picked it, way down in Alabama, where I was born. He told everyone that his baby was a little princess who'd grow up to be special and important, like a queen. He saw a book about famous people once and he liked the picture of Cleopatra."

Miss Cather nodded. "A creative way to choose a name, I'd say. Rather like Samuel Clemens. And you, Holmes, with your unfortunate tendency to snicker. How do you suppose your parents came to choose the name Elmer?"

"I don't know, ma'am."

Phil Foreman, sitting next to him, said, "Probably set him down next to a tree and said, 'Is that an elm or what?'"

Everyone laughed, including Miss Cather. After frowning at his friend, Elmer Holmes joined in.

They talked about the assigned Twain short story, then listened as their teacher described her expectations about their writing.

"I've told you this frequently, but it bears repeating. You must write precisely, depending on close, accurate observations. Try to make your work evolve from your own experiences."

She looked around the room. "Each time I say that some of you look puzzled. I'll try to offer an example."

She was silent for a while, looking at her students; her gaze fell on Molly and a smile curved her lips. "Suppose you are working in a store, any kind of store. For the sake of illustration, let's make it an egg store. One afternoon you're busy attending to your tasks when a customer enters. You approach her politely, trying to do your job, but she's not interested in buying eggs. Instead, she demands to see the chickens that lay them."

None of her classmates, listening to Miss Cather, looked at Molly. Only Cleo would make the connection, but Molly's face still burned. Head down, she tried to be invisible.

"You explain that you know little about chickens, but the woman is relentless. Bothersome as she is, she's a customer and the owner has repeatedly told you the customer is always right."

Molly forgot her self-consciousness and looked up at Miss Cather.

"What are you to do? The woman's impossible, rude and persistent. You'd like to tell her to get out but, of course, you can't. You try to humor her, explaining that the owner could answer her questions, but he's not there and you're only an employee.

"Does that stop her? No. Not only does she keep pestering but she begins snooping in all the corners of the store, then has the nerve to come behind the counter and head towards the back of the shop and the alley behind it. She approaches the rear door, still babbling about finding the hens who laid the eggs."

Miss Cather surveyed her class, gazing briefly at Molly who, like the others, was absorbed in the tale.

"As soon as she opens the door and steps forward to peer out, you're struck by inspiration. You push the door as if to shut it, and she lurches forward. To your intense satisfaction, she's landed in the chicken coop, covered with feathers and sliding on bird droppings. Exactly the fate she deserves."

The class laughed and applauded.

"Granted, you haven't necessarily had an experience like that, but I'm certain yours are at least as interesting; if not, try embellishing them to make them so. Please start your essays now and finish them at home this evening. I'll collect them at the beginning of class tomorrow. Miss Klein and Miss Payson, see me after class."

When the others left , the girls stayed in their classroom.

"Molly, I hope you liked my story and that you would have put that customer in her place."

"I'm not sure I could, but I know the store owner would have."

Willa Cather stared at her, then laughed heartily. Molly understood that, in her own way, her teacher had apologized.

"I wanted to ask about Victor Morelli," she told them. "He's not very interested in literature, but I like his spirit and sense of humor. Mr. Brownell's especially concerned about his finest student. Morelli's your friend and I thought you would know if there's some problem."

Molly and Cleo exchanged glances. Cleo's look meant Molly ought to explain.

Clearing her throat, Molly began. "Victor won't be coming back to Central. He's quit school and is learning to be a stonemason, working with his father and uncles."

"What? That's outrageous!" Miss Cather fumed. "He's wasting his talents."

"His family believes it's best," Molly answered, carefully.

"I must discuss this with Mr. Brownell," Miss Cather said. "He'll have to persuade the Morellis that it's a terrible mistake."

"No, you can't," Molly said, her voice loud in the quiet room. "You mustn't shame them."

Her teacher stared at her, eyes seeming to penetrate Molly's brain. "Vittorio told you that?"

Molly nodded, her misery over her talk with Victor returning.

After a long pause her teacher spoke again. "I see," she said softly. "We mustn't be disrespectful of the Morellis. Still, there has to be a way . . ." Her voice trailed off. "I need to think about this and you two better get to your next class. Before you go, I'd like to invite you to tea on Sunday, at the house where I live with my friend Miss McNary and her family. It's in the East End, on Murray Lane. Do you know where that is?"

"No, ma'am," Cleo said, surprised by the invitation.

"I'll draw a map for you. It's easy enough to find. Do you have bicycles?"

Cleo and Molly, caught off guard, looked at each other, then shook their heads.

"Do you, Miss Cather?" Cleo asked, curiosity getting the better of her.

"Yes. I often cycle to school from the East End. When I worked as an editor I used to ride to the office every day, whatever the weather. But, I don't like to arrive at school on a rainy day all mussed and soggy, so when the weather's unpredictable I take the streetcar."

She looked at her students. "You can do that, too. I should've realized that in many families there are needs more pressing than bicycles."

Molly was confused. To her, pressing was for wrinkled clothes. She'd ask Cleo later.

"Go along, now. I'll give you directions to the house by street-car tomorrow. Remember, Sunday at three o'clock. Mrs. McNary dislikes tardiness as much as I."

Willa Cather liked to invite her best students to the McNary house. The young people learned from visiting a world different from their own, a part of Pittsburgh where families lived in big houses filled with paintings, luxurious furniture, and grand pianos. She believed such visits enhanced their understanding of the importance of gracious manners and self-improvement.

Their teacher was grateful for the opportunities she'd enjoyed since coming to Pittsburgh. Her first job, working as an editor for *Home Monthly,* had soon bored her. Writing about children's teeth and the habits of Angora cats was hardly a challenge. Even her story in class today, to let Molly Klein know she regretted her behavior at the poultry store, was more creative than her magazine work had been.

The best part of her second job, at a newspaper, writing headlines and correcting reporters' copy, was the extra assignment as a drama critic. She regularly saw plays and interviewed actors and important theater people who came to town.

In teaching she'd found work she truly enjoyed, as well as challenges like her current preoccupation with Victor Morelli. Somehow, he had to continue his math studies, finish high school, and attend a university.

Family pride, the girls had hinted, was the issue. She understood that. As a child in Nebraska, she'd seen immigrant families humiliated by the snubs and condescension of local people. She thought of her favorite neighbor, Mr. Schneider, who'd come to Red Cloud from Germany and knew more about operas than anyone she'd ever met. He'd taught her, a young girl homesick for the lush landscape of Virginia and miserable in the bleak prairie, to find comfort in the lyrical music of Verdi.

When he returned to the farmhouse after long days in the fields Mr. Schneider forgot his weariness by playing arias on the battered piano he'd bought from a farmer who moved to Lincoln. He'd tell opera stories to Willa and her friend, Greta, his youngest daughter, then play the melodies the characters sang in the opera, often singing along and inviting them to join him.

Sometimes, when he'd go into town to buy farm supplies, he'd take her and Greta in his wagon. Even now, years later, Willa recalled her anger at the shabby treatment he received from the townspeople. "So, vat you vant, Dutch?" a storekeeper would say in an ugly parody of his accent, often mispronouncing Helmut, his name, or speaking slowly and loudly as if that was the only way he could understand. How stupid and insensitive some of the townspeople were to immigrant families. She knew it had hurt Greta and her father, although they never spoke about it. Just as Molly and Cleo had said—they'd been shamed.

She mustn't do that to the Morellis. She sighed as she collected her books and left the room. She'd find Philip Brownell and explain. He, a kind but naive man, knew much about mathematics but little of the world beyond the classroom and would want to go immediately to Victor's house, pound on the door, and demand that the boy return to school.

For Molly and Cleo, Miss Cather's invitation to tea dominated their thoughts.

What would they wear, how should they act, what do people talk about at a tea? Certainly their families didn't know.

At school the next day, Cleo told Molly her father's reaction. "He said, 'See, just like I been telling you, baby. You're destined for big things; more people than your teacher someday goin' to treat you like a queen.' And you should've heard Granny. She let out a scream everybody in the building heard and two big tears rolled down her cheeks."

"I thought she'd be happy," Molly said, puzzled.

"She was. She kept talking about how no one down home could believe a poor colored girl from Alabama'd be having tea with high society white folks in a big, fancy house. She said it made moving away from her kin and coming North worth it." Cleo shook her head. "I never did see Granny carry on like that before. She got out the Sunday tablecloth—the one she crocheted in Alabama—to put on the table for supper. She said I had to get used to fine things, now that I was mixing with the fanciest families. Daddy and I just stared at her and he said she was fussing more than a girl steppin' out with her first boyfriend.

"Then she started fretting about what I should wear. When I left this morning she was cutting out a dress from the flowered material she laid aside for Easter dinner clothes at church. I guess tea at Miss Cather's house is just as special."

"It's not Miss Cather's house. She only lives there because it belongs to her friend's family. Our teacher's not a rich society lady like your grandmother thinks." Molly heard the peevishness in her own voice. She was jealous of Cleo's new dress and a grandmother who put away pretty fabrics for special occasions. Ashamed, she said, "You'll look nice in your new dress."

"And you in your new blouse," Cleo answered, turning to her. "You shouldn't look so surprised. You know how Granny is when she makes up her mind. When she says you need to have something new, sure as shootin' you get something new. No use to fight it. You'll have a yellow blouse with lace collar and cuffs and a brown bow. Granny says it'll look good with your brown eyes and dark hair and you should wear it with your brown skirt."

When Molly started to protest that it was too much trouble for her to do in a few days, Cleo stopped her. "No use fussing, girl. Once she decides something, Granny won't change her mind. No way, no how. She said to tell you the blouse will be ready Thursday and you should come get it after school."

Molly nodded. If she tried to speak she'd sound as if she was holding back tears. She knew she didn't have to say anything about how grateful she was.

At the boarding house, near the room she shared with her mother, she heard Uncle Abe's voice mingling with Hannah's in the odd mix of Yiddish and Polish that was their conversation. Molly's reminders to speak English went unheeded, despite her mother's increasing fluency and her uncle's comfort with the language. In the store, Uncle Abe surprised her with his blending of English with Polish, German, Italian, or Yiddish, depending on his customer's background.

Once, when she'd asked him how he knew so many languages, he'd laughed.

"I don't. With all kinds of customers, you learn a few words of this and that language, enough to do business. That's all I know, a few words, this and that." He'd laughed again. "I fooled you into thinking I'm smarter than I really am."

This afternoon he wasn't laughing. He and Hannah were arguing. She took a deep breath, preparing to play peacemaker, but her uncle stormed out as she reached for the doorknob.

"Sometimes that mother of yours is impossible," he shouted. "She fools people because she's quiet but she's as stubborn and hard-headed as . . ." He paused, looking at her and permitting himself a small smile, "as you are. Talk some sense into her. I locked the store to bring her home, she was so upset, but I have to get back there."

"You locked the store to bring her home!" Molly's face turned chalky. "Is she sick? Has something terrible happened?"

"No, nothing like that. Something good, only she's too foolish to see it." He hurried off, leaving her baffled.

Her mother was sitting on the bed, holding a letter she extended to Molly. It was from her father, written in Polish, mixed with simple English he'd laboriously learned and taught to the rest of them. Sometimes Molly forgot how scholarly her father was, how he studied before he went to bed, and how determined he'd been that his family learn English to be ready when the time came to leave Poland.

When she'd finished reading Papa's letter, Molly looked at her mother, puzzled. "I don't know why you're upset. Simon's getting married. Isn't that good news? He's old enough—twenty—the girl's related to your friends, the Mazurs, and Papa says everyone's happy. Shouldn't you be, too?"

Her mother glared at her. "You sound like Abe. Think what this means. The girl's from Minsk, in Russia, only visiting the Mazurs. Her father's a furrier who wants your brother to be in the business with him."

"I read that," Molly answered, beginning to feel annoyed. "Isn't that good, that Simon will have a trade and be independent?"

"He'll have a trade in Minsk, not Pittsburgh, if he marries this girl."

Mama sounded irritable; her eyes glittered. Now Molly understood. Simon would move to Minsk to work with his father-in-law, instead of coming to America. Hannah's family would be separated forever.

Molly sat on the bed beside her and put her arm around shoulders that felt bony and frail. "Simon's a grown man," she said in a quiet voice she hoped was soothing. "He makes his own decisions and it sounds, from Papa's letter, like he's happy and certain he wants to marry Sonia."

A pretty name, Molly thought, and imagined that the girl, too, was pretty. Her oldest brother was tall, with merry blue eyes and curly black hair. He must have grown even more handsome since she'd last seen him. In Swidnik her friends' older sisters found excuses to visit her house so they could see Simon. They'd smile up at him, speak softly, and blush.

Hannah Klein knew that her daughter's words made sense, but that didn't ease the hurt. "I'll never see my son again. He'll be gone from me as sure as if he died, God forbid. I won't know his children, my own grandchildren. How can I stand it?"

Molly reached over to wipe away her tears, searching for comforting words. "Maybe he and Sonia will decide to come to America, too, and we'll all be together."

Her mother shook her head. "It doesn't work like that. She's a Russian citizen and Simon's papers have to come from Poland. No, he'll live in Minsk, become part of her family, and Papa and David will come without him. That's the way it has to be. Abe says I should be glad my boy's marrying into a good family, a prosperous family, and won't need to worry about how to make a living." She shrugged. "That's true, but he'll be gone and it breaks my heart."

Molly stroked her mother's hand, unable to answer. Saying they could go to see him in Russia or that Simon and his wife would visit America would be a lie. The family, once reunited here, would never go back to Europe. Simon and his Sonia, no matter how much they'd like to visit, were unlikely to be allowed travel visas, even if they could afford the trip. Russia, like Poland, had special, cruel laws for Jews.

She adored her brother but they'd been separated a long time and, because he was older, they hadn't been as close as she and David. Molly's memories of Simon had dimmed but the reality of never seeing him again saddened her. How much worse her mother must feel.

"You'll write to Simon and his new family, the way you do with Papa and the boys. I know it's not the same, but you don't feel less close to Papa because you write to him instead of talking."

"But I'll see him again," she said, voice trembling. Hannah grew quiet and Molly knew her mother was struggling to be strong.

"Enough. Abe's right that this marriage is a good thing for Simon. We'll write to each other and after Papa and David come and are settled, we'll have photographs taken to send to Simon and Sonia. They'll do the same." She wiped at her eyes again and attempted a smile. "So, tell me about school, and what's going on. We had no time to talk yesterday, I was so late getting home from the Settlement House."

Molly brightened. When she'd explained about the invitation Hannah was happily distracted.

"How will you get there? Is it very far away?"

"Not really. We'll go by streetcar, with directions from Miss Cather. And you'll never guess how Miss Cather travels to school in good weather—on a bicycle!"

Hannah's startled expression made Molly smile. "It's all right for ladies to do that in America? At home people would be shocked. The whole town would gossip."

"What lady in Swidnik could afford a bicycle?" Molly said.

Her mother laughed, the earlier sadness put aside.

"Anyhow, Miss Cather doesn't care what other people think. She does what she wants. She told Cleo and me that when she worked for a magazine publisher she rode her bicycle to the office every day. Sometimes, she said, she raced the streetcars."

Mrs. Klein's eyes widened. "She is most—what is the word I just learned—Oh, I remember! Unusual."

Molly nodded. "She's a good teacher and everyone likes her. We try harder to do well in her class than the others, where the teachers don't seem to care as much."

"It's nice of her to invite you to her party. I'll wash and iron that pretty blouse Cleo's grandmother made for you."

"I'm getting another new one. Mrs. Payson's making me a yellow blouse trimmed with lace. She says it'll be ready in a day or two."

"She's so good to you, Molly. I wish I could do something for them. Maybe ask Mrs. Levin if I can use the kitchen and make a special meal. I could get a fat chicken from the store, roast it, and invite the Paysons to dinner in the dining room, downstairs."

Her mother was a much better cook than Mrs. Levin, but they ate in the dining room with the other boarders because the cost was included in their rent.

"We could invite Miss Cather, too. Especially if she promises to come on her bicycle!"

NINE

Resplendent in new clothes, Molly and Cleo left the Hill District early on the afternoon of the tea party. They consulted Miss Cather's instructions, boarded a streetcar, transferred to another, and arrived promptly at the quiet, tree-lined street.

"These houses are bigger than I ever saw," Molly said. "Look at those porches, with furniture on them! That porch has more room than the first floor of the boarding house."

"No puddles or horse manure on the street," Cleo said. "No wooden barrels or fruit crates on the sidewalk. I guess folks don't build fires outside in winter. Must be mighty boring."

Molly laughed. "Maybe that's why Miss Cather rides her bicycle to school—for the excitement."

"You ask her that, girl. I won't." Cleo looked at the slip of paper in her hand. "This is the address she gave us. Must be the right place."

The door bell was answered by a young woman not much older than the two girls, wearing a long gray dress covered by a crisp white apron.

"Please come in," she said and led them into a large, brightly-lit vestibule where they waited uncertainly, hearing muted laughter and the hum of conversation.

"Molly, Cleo, welcome," said their teacher, walking towards them, hands outstretched. She looked much the same as at school, dressed in a neat green frock, her hair pinned into a bun.

"I'd like you to meet my friend, Miss McNary, and her parents. These are the good people who've included me in their household."

She led them to a stately older couple who smiled, shook their hands, and introduced them to their daughter, Elizabeth.

Slender and quite pretty, Elizabeth McNary was taller than Willa Cather, and more elaborately dressed. She wore a lavender gown with lace at the collar and adorning the full, billowing sleeves. Blonde ringlets framed her oval face.

She extended her hand, which felt soft and smooth in Molly's. "I'm always happy to meet Willa's students. She often speaks about her classes."

"Molly and Cleo are two of my prize pupils," their teacher said. "I think they'll be surprised to see another of their friends here."

With that, she led them across a large room, the floor so thickly carpeted that their footsteps were inaudible, to a cluster of chairs upholstered in velvet and arranged near a small table covered with a lace cloth. On it was a silver vase filled with red and yellow roses.

Molly was so fascinated with her surroundings it was a while before she noticed the occupant of one of the chairs.

"Victor!" she said, a little louder than was proper.

Cleo gaped.

"I knew you'd be pleased to see Vittorio," Miss Cather said. "This lady with him is Miss Helen Bauman."

Molly stared at the face that belonged with the familiar name. Before she could speak, Miss Bauman took her hand and shook it.

"Although we haven't met, I know a great deal about this young lady. Her mother is my friend and one of the best students at the Settlement House. And this must be Cleo, about whom I've also heard many good things."

Cleo smiled and shook her hand while Molly stammered, "But . . . but how do you know . . ."

"Vittorio? I didn't until this afternoon, but Miss Cather told me about him, particularly his math abilities. And your mother mentioned him as well, so I felt I already knew him, too."

"And Miss Cather?" Cleo said.

"That's quite another story. Why don't you get some tea, join us, and I'll tell you all about it."

"And I must go mingle with the other guests. Please excuse me." With a wave and what Molly recognized as the self-satisfied smile she'd sometimes noticed in class, Miss Cather disappeared.

Molly and Cleo moved to the dining room where they saw a huge table draped in lace and laden with platters of tiny sandwiches, an array of pastries, fruits, and candies. Seated at one end of the table, Mrs. McNary presided over a silver tea service that glowed in the soft light from a crystal chandelier. Molly studied the rainbow of colors shimmering in the glass prisms, trying to memorize every detail so she could describe this house to her mother.

After thanking Mrs. McNary for the tea she poured into a thin porcelain cup covered with blue flowers, the saucer painted with gold leaves, Molly chose three diamond-shaped sandwiches of thin white bread, filled with a chopped green mixture she couldn't identify. She added two chocolate cookies and some fat red grapes to her plate and moved to the side to wait for Cleo.

Near her, a plump woman in a long purple dress and matching, feathered hat spoke to a mustached man Molly thought looked like a gray shadow. "So generous of the McNarys," the woman said in a voice intended as a whisper, "to include that impertinent young woman in everything."

"Who d'you mean, my dear?" her companion said in a tone that matched his look.

"That Cather woman, from the West. She wants to be a writer, I hear, although right now she's teaching at that dreary high school on the Hill. I understand she quit her first editing job because the magazine wasn't highbrow enough."

"Mmph," muttered the man while Molly strained to hear.

"She's no paragon of refinement herself, you understand. The woman has a sharp tongue and no qualms about criticizing the city. The last time I was here I overheard her say that Pittsburgh is divided into two parts, Presbyteria and Bohemia, and the former is much the larger and more influential kingdom. What gall! She even joked about Mr. Carnegie's generosity, describing him as Holy St. Andrew and Pittsburgh as a city of dreadful dirt where what we care about most are coal and iron mills and big houses on Fifth Avenue. She probably writes that drivel in the articles she sends back to the Wild West. Now really!"

"Cheeky, is she?" the man answered, but Molly saw that he almost smiled.

"Indeed. And look at the riffraff she invites here. Students of hers, I understand, immigrant whelps, even colored. The McNarys certainly are broad-minded to put up with it all. One would think they'd worry about their silver being stolen."

Cleo joined Molly and the woman and her companion moved away. Molly turned to watch, scowling.

"What'd they do, step on your toes?" Cleo said.

"I wish I'd stepped on theirs," Molly answered. "Never mind. They're mean, nasty people, criticizing Miss Cather."

Victor, joining them, said, "She wouldn't care. Other people's opinions don't bother her." He described his mother's reaction when their teacher stopped at his house to invite him to tea. "The signorina was on a bicycle," his mother told him. "I stare, but she only smile and say give Vittorio her note."

Remembering, Victor laughed. "Mama couldn't stop talking about it. She said the neighbors gossiped all day about the strange American lady."

"Were you as surprised as we were to be invited here?" Molly asked, wondering where to put down her plate. However high class the green filling in the sandwiches was, she didn't like it. The servant who'd answered the door approached and took the plate, almost before Molly could snatch back the cookies.

"I thought she'd lecture me about quitting school, but not at all. In the note she said my friends would be here and someone else she wanted me to meet."

"I'm glad you came," Cleo said. "We hardly see you." She looked around. "It's kind of hard to talk here, though. Too many people acting high and mighty."

"Was it Miss Bauman she wanted you to meet?" Molly said.

Victor nodded. "Nice lady. She's a social worker at the Settlement House. I didn't know what that meant, but she said her job's to solve problems for people in the neighborhood."

"My mother says she helps lots of people," Molly said. "Because of Miss Bauman she's getting much better at English and not so shy about speaking it. Miss Bauman got her into a class that starts after she leaves the store and sometimes even meets with her alone so Mama can practice new words in conversation."

"The lady has an idea for me, too," Victor explained. "At the Settlement House night school, people study all kinds of subjects after work, not just English. They learn job skills, like typing and bookkeeping."

"Do you want to study typing?" Cleo said, surprised.

Victor's laugh was loud in the room; several people turned to look. "I hate to think what my uncles'd say about that! Miss Bauman told me I can finish my high school courses at night and study math there. Wouldn't that be great?"

"You don't need any old math, Victor. You're ready for the special genius stuff, the kind you were doing with Mr. Brownell," Cleo said.

"It won't matter. If I can take the courses I need to earn my diploma, maybe I'll find a way to study the more complicated ones later."

"Could you do all that and still work?" Molly said.

"Miss Bauman says people of all ages are doing it, so why couldn't I? After work I'll wash up, grab some food, and go to the Settlement House. Your mother does that, doesn't she?"

"Yes, but that's because Uncle Abe lets her leave early when the store isn't busy, or else I fill in so she can go to her classes."

Victor's chin came up the way it did when he'd made up his mind. "I'll manage. I can't leave work early, but if I have to, I'll go straight to class without going home. My family'll have to understand. If they don't, that's too bad."

His friends said nothing more. Molly realized how lucky she and Cleo were; their families insisted they attend school, even on days when they didn't feel like it.

Cleo bit into one of the tiny sandwiches and made a face. "What's in these things? It tastes like something cows would munch."

"Close," said a voice behind them, followed by a familiar laugh. "It's watercress," Miss Cather explained, "an expensive weed that grows near streams. I prefer roast beef myself."

Standing beside her was a tall, slender man dressed in a dark suit with matching vest and flowing crimson tie. He was smiling, so Cleo wasn't too embarrassed by her remark about the sandwiches.

"Here's someone you'll like much better than watercress. This is my friend, Mr. Ethelbert Nevin, a famous composer and pianist. He and his family live out in the country in a beautiful house called Vinacre. Sometimes I'm lucky enough to be invited there and listen to him playing his own music."

"Do you go there on your bicycle?" Molly said, surprised when the adults laughed at her reasonable question.

"Knowing your teacher's tenacity, I believe she would if she had to, but fortunately she can take a train," Mr. Nevin said.

Willa looked at him, eyes bright with amusement. "I shouldn't tease about tenacity if I were you." She turned to her students. "Mr. Nevin told me that when he was a music student in Italy he was desperate to get a special piano to his studio up in the Tuscan hills. The studio was a converted stable, remote from roads and transportation. That didn't stop Ethelbert. He persuaded some farmers from the nearest village to haul a grand piano over old trails to his donkey stable. They stayed, drinking grappa, and listening to him play. They probably sang along with the pianist!"

"Indeed they did," the composer answered. "We started with Neapolitan street songs—they didn't know them, but they were quick learners—and ended with arias from *Madame Butterfly.*"

"You must've paid those *paesanos* big money," Victor said, "to pull that piano up into the hills."

"Not really," said Mr. Nevin. "They liked the challenge to their wagon, their donkey, and their skills. When they made it, that was reason for a celebration. And celebrate we did!"

"With Ethelbert, it's any excuse for a party," Miss Cather added. "I was visiting at Vinacre when another guest was celebrating his birthday. He was serenaded all day long."

"And toasted with *grappa*? That's what we'd do," Victor said. "Sometimes, when my uncles can find the right kinds of grapes, they make it for holidays. Italians like parties, too."

"So does your teacher," Mr. Nevin said. "She recently went on an evening boat excursion for thirty miles along the Ohio

River. She and her friends were entertained with banjo music and dinner, then sailed back in the dark, admiring the lights of the city."

"More like the red glare from the steel mills, but it was a dramatic sight," Miss Cather said. She looked at the young people. "Mr. Nevin rarely sees my serious side, so he doesn't understand how hard we work in class."

"We do," Cleo said, "Miss Cather makes us write every day and she's strict. Once she told us the art of writing is like a game of tennis. You had to hit the ball as hard as possible, but keep it within lines or boundaries to make a success of it."

"In the Polish village where I come from," Molly said, "nobody ever heard of tennis, so I didn't know what Miss Cather was talking about. But when she explained, I understood," Molly added.

"There's very little these three don't understand, Ethelbert. I wish you could teach them music, as well," their teacher said.

"I know about music, and so does Victor," Cleo said. "He plays the violin at parties and my father performs in a club."

"I'd like to know more about that," Mr. Nevin said. "What does he play?"

"The piano, and he's really good. He plays ragtime at the Southern Club, not far from where we live."

"Does he have a regular club date, a night when people know to come hear him?" the composer asked.

"No sir. It depends on his shifts. My daddy works in the Homestead mill, sometimes nights and sometimes the day turn. My grandmother says his schedule's like putting together puzzle pieces."

"I surely would like to hear him. Ragtime's wonderful when it's played well. Could we come to the Southern Club sometime, Miss Cather and I, when he's scheduled to play?"

Cleo squirmed and looked at the floor. "I'd have to ask. It's . . ." She hesitated. "White folks don't usually go there."

Miss Cather reached out and gently lifted Cleo's chin so she was looking directly into her eyes. "We'd be honored to come if it's all right with your father." Miss Cather turned to Victor. "Of course, we'd be happy to hear you, too, Vittorio, but I don't think we can invite ourselves to private parties and weddings, even for the privilege of your performance."

"I'm not so good, anyhow. Mostly, I play loud. When the guests are toasting with *grappa* they don't notice my mistakes."

Miss Cather and her friend drifted away to talk with other guests and Cleo and Molly decided it was time to leave.

Victor agreed. They found Mrs. McNary, still presiding at the tea table, and thanked her. Cleo noticed there were plenty of green-filled sandwiches left. She was not the only one who thought they tasted like weeds.

As they were leaving, they waved goodbye to Miss Bauman, who was sitting with several women in brightly colored dresses. She called out, "Vittorio, I expect to see you soon. Don't disappoint me."

"No, ma'am," he answered and they walked out, along the tree-lined avenue to the streetcar stop.

On the way home they went over the details of the party. They all agreed the food wasn't much, but the house and the neighborhood were beautiful.

"Maybe rich people don't care what food tastes like, as long as it looks fancy," Cleo said. "They have so much else on their minds they probably think food's boring."

"What would they have on their minds?" Victor scoffed. "How to spend their money? When they go home after a tea party, they must go straight to the ice box to eat the leftovers."

"You're talking foolish. Rich people don't have leftovers," Cleo said. "Their servants throw away what they don't eat, or eat it themselves. And I don't think society folks like the McNarys spend much time in their kitchen looking in their ice boxes."

"Too bad," Victor said. "They miss a lot."

Molly said, "My mother'll be surprised when I tell her Miss Bauman was at the party. I'd like her job, helping people and going to fancy houses, too."

"You just did and we decided the food's better in our own neighborhood," Cleo said.

"No, silly. Be a social worker. I think I'd like that more than being a teacher."

"I wouldn't be so sure," Cleo answered. "Miss Cather gets to live in the fancy house, not just go to parties there."

Molly sighed. "You know what I mean. Besides, teachers have to put up with kids like you and Victor, and that's worse than eating weed sandwiches."

When all the guests had departed from the McNary house, Willa Cather climbed the stairs to the tiny third floor sewing room that'd been converted to her study. She liked the coziness of the space; it reminded her of her bedroom in Red Cloud. As a teenager, she'd worked in a store and saved enough money to buy floral wallpaper for her room. She'd retreat there to read and dream about being a writer.

Sitting at her desk in another secluded room devoted to writing, she wondered about the dreams of the three young people who'd been her guests.

Their dreams would be harder to attain. Two of them had to reshape the worlds of their European families into their own American lives. The other, a descendant of slaves, was uneasy about bringing white strangers into a place intended for her own people. She had to find her way in a world divided into black and white.

Their teacher sighed, thinking about Vittorio's inevitable clashes with his family about the Settlement House and finishing his high school studies. And there was Molly, whose English surpassed her mother's, embracing her life here while her mother resisted.

Cleo's father was undoubtedly having his problems, too, working long shifts at the Homestead Works. Willa remembered her tour of that mill, soon after arriving in Pittsburgh. Stumbling through a haze of heat and grime, straining to hear her guide above a roar like an inferno, she'd watched flames shooting from the tops of blast furnaces. The machinery towered over the laborers scurrying like ants below.

She thought about the twelve hour shifts the men worked and the weariness that stole time for their families and, for William Payson, music. Reaching for the file where she kept copies of articles she'd sent to the Nebraska newspaper, she searched for the one about Pottersville, in Homestead, where some of the mill workers lived.

It was, she'd written,

> *a collection of some sixty or seventy hovels made of thin planks and painted red, huddled in the soot and ashes and cinder heaps back of one of the rolling mills and inside the fifteen-foot stockade which surrounds the town-front of the steel mill.*

She'd described one six-room boarding house that

> *reported 70 inmates, some rooms accommodating 20 lodgers. This was made possible by the twelve hour shift system. Every bed does double duty and every floor is a bed. One set of men get up, go to work; another set, tired and dirty, creep into the same sheets and go to sleep.*

In the same article she'd written,

> *The whiskey drunk in Homestead every Saturday night would float an ocean steamer.*

She stared out of her window at the serene neighborhood beneath her and considered the contrasts in this city she'd begun to think of as home: below was a broad street lined with trees that offered a canopy of shade all summer long. The poor wretches of Pottersville baked in summer and would soon shiver in bone-numbing cold as winter closed in.

Her friends back in Nebraska would find her life here hard to imagine. Before starting to teach, when she'd worked at the newspaper, she had interviewed the famous Rudyard Kipling and sent home a copy of the article. She'd also sent the one she'd written about her meeting with the bandmaster and composer, John Philip Sousa. Her parents' letters described how proud of her they were.

She wrote to her friends about the concerts she attended at Carnegie Hall, the ornate space that filled with men in formal clothes and women in long satin and brocade gowns. She described dinners at the Schenley Hotel, the endless courses of food, the varieties of wines, the meals that went on for hours.

To her friend, Elizabeth McNary, she grumbled about leaving lavish parties to step back into the drizzling, dripping Pittsburgh night with the infernal glare of the iron furnaces flaunting itself across the sky.

Elizabeth had laughed at her complaints. "Last week it was the symphony conductor, that jolly Victor Herbert, you were fussing about. As I recall, you said that 'asking Mr. Herbert for inspired composition was like asking for champagne at a mutton shop.'"

Willa, chuckling, had responded, "Clever. I must include that in one of my articles."

She knew the city was good for her, seminal to her writing. Some short stories based on Pittsburgh experiences and people she'd come to know had begun to take hazy shape in her mind. Teaching was much more gratifying and challenging than she'd expected and offered rich raw material for future stories. Perhaps, she thought, as she replaced the folder in her desk drawer, Molly, Cleo, and Vittorio would make their way into her fiction as well.

TEN

Hannah Klein wasn't back from work when her daughter returned. Restless, Molly wandered around their room, trying to persuade herself to study.

In a neat stack on the bed were the last letters Nathan Klein had sent; her mother must've been rereading them before going to the store. Molly held the thin sheets of stationery in her hand, looking at the small, neat handwriting crowding the pages. The script was like her father, a man who enjoyed reading and learning more than being a shopkeeper.

He and her mother had married young; Mama was only eighteen when Simon, soon to be a bridegroom himself, was born. Two children died in infancy before David's birth. She, the baby, came along three years later. Memories of growing up in the small rooms behind the store were happy, but Molly knew her parents struggled every day, not only against poverty, but also fear that the government would impose harsh new laws to make their lives even harder.

The Jews of Swidnik could never feel completely at home in their village. Polish authorities regularly reminded them that they were strangers, not real Poles but intruders in the land, allowed to stay only because of the "kindness" of the government. It did not matter that Molly's ancestors had lived in Poland for many generations, earning their living and obeying the laws. Because they had different religious beliefs and customs, Jews were often mistreated: they could only live in one part of the town, they paid extra taxes, they couldn't own farms or buy property outside of their tiny community. Sometimes they were demeaned and cursed when they had to venture outside their neighborhood. Occasionally, they were physically attacked; boys on the way to school were beaten by gangs of thugs.

Yet, when the opportunity came to leave for America, Hannah protested, hating the idea of leaving her husband and sons. At night, when they thought Molly was asleep, she'd heard her parents' whispered arguments. Her father, usually mild and compliant, had been adamant.

"You have to go and take our little girl while there's a chance to get away. You know the future here—scraping for a living, afraid of what the peasants might do to us if the government demands more taxes or their crops are bad. They'll blame us for their troubles, like always, and life will only get worse. You and Molly must leave while you can."

"What about you and the boys? How can I bear to leave you, my husband? And David needs me, he's still a little boy. Simon's nearly grown, but David?"

"We'll come to America when we can, you know that. While we're waiting, we'll manage, we'll take care of each other. I'll learn to cook. So I won't be as good as you, but we'll eat."

The sound from her mother had been half-laugh, half-sob. Molly hadn't heard anything more.

A few weeks later, Mr. Gelman, a shoemaker in their village, was beaten by a drunken farmer when he asked for payment for mending the man's shoes. The police were called but refused to jail the farmer, claiming Mr. Gelman provoked him by demanding too much money.

That night, as their neighbors muttered about scapegoats and bigotry they were helpless to change, Hannah finally agreed. Life in Swidnik would never improve; she and Molly would leave for Pittsburgh, where Uncle Abe would be their sponsor. The rest of the family would put their names on a waiting list and join them when their turn came.

She missed her father and brothers, but Molly felt increasingly at home in America. Her life in the old country was a vague memory, her father's letters like stories from a book filled with names to which she could no longer assign faces. She hoped her brother's new life with Sonia in Minsk would be better and easier than his days in Swidnik. She suspected Simon hoped so, too.

Molly wanted to introduce David to a new life here. She thought of her brother's sense of fun, his easy laughter and quick way of making friends that would smooth his adjustment to a new world. For her father, reuniting with his wife and daughter would be enough. What work he'd do here she didn't know, but brash and outspoken Uncle Abe would undoubtedly arrange something.

If only they'd come soon, Molly thought, the tightness in her chest reminding her that it could be a long time before her family got permission to emigrate. No wonder Mama was often sad, despite Papa's gossipy, cheery messages.

Molly fingered the pages of the most recent letter, much of it about the plans for Simon's wedding. Papa and David had been granted permission by their district's governor to travel to Minsk for the ceremony. It wouldn't be easy—the long train ride was expensive—but they were determined to go. Papa's cousin, Carl, who lived in the next town, would come to Swidnik to tend the tailoring shop. Papa and David would stay with relatives of the bride for three days. Her father ended the letter by promising to write all the details of the wedding so she and Mama would feel as if they'd been there.

Molly shook her head as she reread those lines. Dear Papa; he tried so hard to sound optimistic, but he'd have to be a magician to ease his wife's sadness at missing her son's wedding.

The next morning Cleo wasn't waiting outside her boarding house and, because she was late, Molly assumed she'd gone on ahead. It was damp and windy, mist rising from the river to mix with smoke from the soft coal used by Pittsburgh mills. Gray smog hid the weak glimmer of the sun. Lights would be turned on in her classrooms, Molly knew, and the street lamps would be burning in the afternoon when she returned home. One of the best memories she had of Swidnik was blue skies and, in winter, sunlight on clean, white snow.

Ahead, Central High loomed out of the fog, its gray stones topped by two heavy towers, like a sinister castle in a children's story. Inside, she hurried across worn wooden floors to climb three flights of stairs for Miss Cather's class, on the top floor.

Miss Cather hadn't arrived when Molly, with a sigh of relief, slid into her seat near Cleo's. Their teacher disliked tardiness.

"I hope we get our essays back today," Cleo said. "I did what she always says—observe carefully, describe clearly—but I thought I did that last time, too, and I only got an eighty. She's hard to please."

Molly nodded. "I thought mine was good and she gave me an eighty three."

"I hear she never grades above eighty-five, but I aim to keep trying," Cleo said. "Did you memorize a poem?"

"A sonnet from Shakespeare. I don't know what half the words mean, but I think I can say them right. And it's only fourteen lines."

"Everybody I talked to picked a sonnet because they're short. Get ready. Here she comes."

Miss Cather strode into the room. Dressed in a pale blue shirt with white collar and cuffs and a navy blue skirt, she studied the class. She wasn't wearing a colorful tie. Molly wondered if that was a bad sign. Like the others, she nervously waited. Their teacher was merciless in condemning sloppy work and had no patience with slow or lazy students.

At times she embarrassed classmates whose work she deemed inept or mediocre, reading their essays aloud and ridiculing mistakes. Molly decided, if she became a teacher, she would treat all her students the same instead of ridiculing some and inviting others to tea. She'd invite everyone to her parties.

Today Cleo, Molly, and the others felt lucky. After Harry Burton and Ruth Korn recited their passages from *Macbeth* Miss Cather began talking about the importance of poetry, drama, and music in people's lives.

"When I interviewed the famous writer, Mr. Rudyard Kipling, during his visit here, it was a thrilling experience," she told her listeners. "He had great energy and passion for his art. We should follow his example, be stirred by life's artistic adventures. Music and literature should be important to all people. Think of Verdi, the creator of great operas. His music is filled with both love and spirituality, speaking to two of humanity's cardinal needs."

Molly heard exhaled breaths around her. Not always sure what Miss Cather meant, the whole class relaxed when she told stories about her experiences. They were safe for a little while.

"We must admire and respect our neighbors who demonstrate imagination and individuality despite their responsibilities. Think of the people in your lives laboring in the mills and mines who don't allow their spirits to be crushed by brutal work. We should all be very proud of them."

Miss Cather looked around at her students. "Which is not to say that there isn't room for improvement in this very classroom. Listening to you recite your poetry reminded me of returning to America after visiting England, when my countrymen's speech sounded like burrs on sandpaper." She studied her students. "Since Charles Martin scowled at that description, he'll be our next performer. Try, won't you, Martin, not to be another burr."

Blushing, he stood, cleared his throat, and began, "...Uh...Friends, Romans, and countrymen, lend me your ears."

Relaxing time over, Molly and her classmates tried to pay attention.

ELEVEN

By mid-November, a winter chill had settled over the city. On their way home in the late afternoons, Cleo and Molly tried to avoid smoke and sparks from street bonfires. Intended to warm the icy hands and feet of vendors who worked outside, and fed by the empty crates shopkeepers stacked on the sidewalks, the fires added to the layers of smog that made Molly's eyes water and sting.

Crouching near the fire, boys called out or waved to passersby. Some faces were familiar—classmates like Victor, who had quit school to work. Unlike Victor, these boys weren't learning a trade. Most sold newspapers to workers returning to their boarding houses, men who read them slowly after their evening meal and before fatigue made the words swim and blur.

Immigrant laborers used newspapers to practice English and escape from the harshness of their lives. They read about western frontier towns where daring bandits preyed on trains, and prospectors, fighting starvation, struck gold and, overnight, were rich as old-country kings.

The boys near the fire hoped storekeepers would hire them to run errands. They asked for money from umbrella vendors and peddlers of knives and scissors who stopped to warm stiff fingers at the fire before resuming, street by street, their search for customers.

"I'm glad my daddy doesn't have to do that," Cleo said, pointing to a bearded man. Wrinkles in his face deepened into a scowl as, exhaling white puffs of breath, he heaved a bundle to his shoulder. "Daddy works hard in the mill and some of the other men call him names, but at least he makes good money."

"What about his music? Does he get to play at the club?"

"Not much. I forgot to tell Miss Cather he said it would be all right for her and her friend to come hear him."

"Could I come, too?" Molly said.

"I'll ask. I've never been there, either."

Later, when she told her mother about it, Hannah Klein frowned. "It is not proper, young girls in a place like that. People will be drinking. I don't think it's right."

Molly answered, "Cleo's father will be there. And my English teacher with her friend, a famous composer." Her mother's fearfulness annoyed her; why was she always so meek about American ways? "You know Cleo's grandmother wouldn't let her go if it's not all right," she added, not really knowing if Cleo would be allowed to go. "This is America, not Poland, where the police might come and arrest us. Don't act like you just got off the boat."

Hannah shook her head. Sometimes she hardly recognized her outspoken daughter. She'd changed so much in the four years in America and was different from the girls in the village where she was born. They behaved like their mothers before them—never free to do as they chose. Hannah envied Molly's confidence, the easy way she accepted her new freedom, but the changes troubled her, too.

She worried sometimes that Molly's new ways might be dangerous, bringing trouble to the family. What would her husband say If he were here? She could ask Abe, but lately he'd been so busy visiting Bella Bloom, they rarely spoke. When Hannah was in the store he'd usually leave to attend to business matters, gossip with other merchants, or, increasingly, to see Mrs. Bloom.

"I don't know what to tell you, Molly. Now I have to go to my class. I'll talk to Miss Bauman and see what she thinks."

"Can I come with you and tell my side of the story? You might leave something out."

Despite her worry, Hannah smiled. When Molly wanted something, she refused to give up. Hannah was certain her husband would like that, exasperating as it was. "You'll have to hurry. I can't wait while you fix your hair and inspect yourself in the mirror. So you won't look like you just got off the boat?"

"Oh, mother!" Molly said, then put her arm around Hannah as they got their coats and headed for the Settlement House.

As they approached the building, its exterior blackened by smoke and grit from the mills, Molly saw that every room was illuminated. She followed her mother down a long corridor to a room where people of varying ages sat, heads bent over books and tablets as they wrote. At the front of the room, watching their progress, was Miss Bauman. Dressed in a long brown skirt and matching jacket, plainer clothes than she'd worn at the McNarys' party, she was dictating words from a book in her hand. She looked up as Molly and her mother waited in the doorway and came to meet them.

"Hannah, I was wondering where you were. And I see you've brought a visitor. Good evening, Molly."

Molly muttered a greeting, embarrassed to interrupt. "I don't believe you've come here before, have you?"

Molly shook her head.

"Then this is a good opportunity for your mother to practice pronunciation and for me to give you a tour. Hannah, please continue reading these words, beginning with 'schedule.' Your classmates are working at spelling and using the dictionary. If I'm not back by the time you get through the *s*'s and *t*'s, go over the list and spell the words so they can check their answers."

Uncertain, her mother took the book and nodded. Molly and Miss Bauman started down the corridor.

"Your mother's a smart lady, but not sure of herself and her abilities. She's especially good at working with the others. Has she told you she's started some tutoring?"

Miss Bauman noticed Molly's expression. "I see she hasn't. She's doing so well with grammar and language usage that I have her helping some of the newer immigrants. It's good practice for her and encouraging to the recent arrivals to see how well others have done. We could use more help. Do you think you might be interested?"

Caught off guard, Molly hesitated. She'd never thought about coming here; school and helping at the poultry store took a lot of time.

As if reading her mind, Miss Bauman said, "You wouldn't have to commit to a regular schedule, only coming when you find time. It'd be a good experience for you, especially since you're thinking about social work."

"How do you know that?"

"I have my sources," she answered, smiling. "You wouldn't believe me if I used that popular phrase about a little bird telling me, so I'll confess. Not only does your mother tell me about your activities and ideas—and very proudly—but I also ask a friend of yours when I see him. He's here tonight, in a room right up the hall. Shall we look in and say hello?"

They stopped before a closed door. Miss Bauman knocked softly and entered, Molly following. Standing at the blackboard, at work on the most complicated scrawl of math symbols she'd ever seen, were Victor and a teacher.

When both turned, Molly's voice rose. "Mr. Brownell! I didn't know you taught at the Settlement House."

Victor, chalk in hand, grinned at her.

"He doesn't," Miss Bauman explained. "He comes here for four hours every week to work with Vittorio. We're very grateful to him for volunteering."

"It's what I do for fun, Molly. I know that sounds strange to you, since math isn't high on your list of pleasures, but when Victor left Central I had no one else to play with formulas with me." He looked at her and smiled. "I've been waiting for you and Cleo to offer to stay after school and do trigonometry, but so far you girls haven't stepped forward."

Victor laughed. "If they had to choose, they'd probably rather split rocks with me."

"You're right," Molly said. "I have no idea what you're doing with those numbers."

"If it's any comfort, neither do I," Miss Bauman said. "Shall we continue our tour and leave these gentlemen to their peculiar idea of fun?"

"If you're going to be around for a while," Victor said as they turned to leave, "I'll look for you after my class."

"I'll be waiting for my mother in room . . ." She looked at Miss Bauman.

"You'll find her at room 112; you can meet her there."

Before she'd finished speaking, he and Mr. Brownell had returned their attention to the board.

"I didn't realize this was such a big place," Molly said as they passed rooms where people studied and talked together. In one of them young boys were lined up, throwing balls into a net basket mounted on the wall.

"Or that so many activities occur here? Settlement House has changed since I began coming. At first, I was a volunteer. Because I'm a trained nurse, a friend asked me to teach immigrant mothers about good hygiene for their babies. How to bathe them properly, protect their skin from sores, things like that. I started thinking about health problems in older children and realized many of them weren't eating right. Either their parents couldn't afford good food or were spending their hard-earned money on the wrong things. So we started a milk bar and that's been a big success."

"A what?" Molly asked.

"A place where children can come to get free milk, as much of it as they want. Sometimes, when we get contributions from wealthy people, we have fruit, too. The children get to take home an apple or an orange."

Miss Bauman looked off into space, as if she were reliving earlier days. "Early on, I knew that much more had to be done. It wasn't enough to teach new arrivals English, or try to improve their eating habits and hygiene. They needed to have some fun, too, to feel happier with their lives here."

"So you brought in Mr. Brownell to play at math puzzles with people like Victor Morelli," Molly said.

"That's a special case," she answered. Miss Bauman stopped at the entrance to a room painted a soft beige and furnished with a desk, three chairs and four green filing cabinets. "This is my office. We can talk here until you go to room 112."

Molly, choosing a seat facing Miss Bauman, who sat behind her desk, said, "What did you do to help people have fun?"

"That depended on their ages and backgrounds. Most clients—that's what we call our regular visitors—are immigrants. They need to learn the ways of a new country, so our first responsibility was to help them with a strange language and customs. But they all seemed so earnest and serious that I thought they should relax a little. We started organizing games, making spaces for sports, like the room where you saw the basket on the wall.

"We encouraged adults to meet for socializing, not only with their countrymen, but with other immigrants, too. They play cards, or the women knit and crochet together and exchange ideas for solving family problems."

Miss Bauman looked at Molly. "Before I knew it, I was here every day, organizing groups, teaching, taking children to Mr. Carnegie's library to show them how to borrow books. Finally, the good people who provide funds for Settlement House hired me. I even got an official title—social worker."

"Do you like what you do?" Molly said.

"At times it's frustrating and overwhelming and I get tired. But I love it. I can't imagine doing anything more satisfying."

"I think I'd like it, too," Molly said. "I thought I wanted to be a teacher, but being a social worker sounds better."

"It's a little bit of everything, including teaching, but mostly it's about seeing what kind of help people need and trying to provide it. You can go to school and learn all kinds of skills that would help." She looked at Molly. "And if you come to Settlement House to volunteer you'll learn about social work right on the site."

Molly was silent, thinking.

"I know you don't have much spare time, but even a few hours would really help. We always need volunteers at the milk bar, with baby care, or helping older children practice reading. You needn't decide now. Just think about it."

There was a soft knock and the door opened. Miss Bauman looked up and smiled.

"Come in, Hannah. I've just given your daughter a tour. How did the class go?"

"Good," she said, sitting down next to Molly.

"Your mother is one of our success stories," Miss Bauman said. "She says it's because your father insisted your family study English in Poland, but she's too modest about being a very good student."

Hannah's face flushed with pleasure. With a pang, Molly realized her mother rarely heard praise for her work from Uncle Abe and she herself mostly took her mother's activities for granted.

"Molly said earlier that you were troubled about her plan to visit a club with Cleo. Why don't you tell me about it?"

Molly listened as her mother struggled to express her anxiety about whether it would be proper and how the adults at the club would react. She knew Miss Bauman understood.

"I believe what worries you," she said softly, "is that the club is a place where colored people, not whites, usually go."

Her mother nodded, looking uncomfortable. "We had no Negroes in our town," she said, "and I do not understand about what goes on here. Colored and white people are neighbors . . ." She hesitated, searching for words. "We are all poor together, struggling to make a living, yet there's so much separation. Cleo's father had trouble getting hired at the mill, even when he's strong and a good worker. Colored and white people go to different churches, belong to different clubs. Negro ladies clean rich white ladies' houses, but can't get jobs in stores selling the same ladies hats or gloves." Hannah sighed. "I do not understand."

Miss Bauman nodded. "It's hard to explain and it makes me sad to think about it. You know what it was like in Poland, all the cruel things done to your people by those in power. You came to America expecting better, but we do many cruel things here, too. Negro musicians like Mr. Payson play in colored clubs because that's where they're welcome; they're shut out of the white clubs. And chances at better jobs aren't often open to colored folks, either. The clubs and churches were started by people with a lot in common who got together. It was easier and safer than trying to force their way into places where they were made to feel strange and unwelcome—like greenhorns."

She looked at the two faces before her, so similar in their solemnity. "Things will get better. Molly and Cleo already demonstrate that by their friendship. I think going to hear Mr. Payson is a great idea. Why don't you see if you can go, too, Hannah? I bet you'd love it."

Molly thanked Miss Bauman and decided that her visit to the Settlement House had gone very well, indeed. She also realized that Victor, absorbed in his math session with Mr. Brownell, might not be finished for hours. She asked Miss Bauman to tell him she was going home and would see him another time, probably here. Molly already knew that she'd be spending much more time at the Settlement House.

TWELVE

In early December plans to hear William Payson perform were complete. Molly and Cleo would attend with Mrs. Payson, meeting Miss Cather and Mr. Nevin at the Southern Club.

Molly was disappointed when her mother refused to go. "It does not feel right, a place with music I don't understand and so many people I do not know," Hannah said.

When Molly scowled, her mother explained. "People dress up to have a good time. I would be ashamed of how I look—"

She held up a hand to stop Molly from interrupting. "I only have the clothes I wear every day to the store. You'll be pretty in that blouse Mrs. Payson made, but I don't want to meet your teacher in my old black dress. Besides—a place where people go for parties, I would feel strange without Papa."

Now Molly understood. It wasn't the dress, it was her mother's European ideas about respectability. In Swidnik married women didn't go to evening parties without their husbands.

"You're in America," Molly said. "But sometimes you act like a greenhorn. Cleo and her grandmother are friends. Miss Cather will be there and Mr. Nevin, the composer. Don't you want to meet them? What could be more proper?"

Molly couldn't change her mother's mind. The night of the performance she tried again, gave up, and hurried outside to wait with the Paysons for the carriage to the club.

"You look so sweet in that blouse, Molly. I knew it would be a good style for you," Cleo's grandmother said.

Sitting in the carriage, Molly looked at Mrs. Payson, beautiful in her silky, deep purple dress. A pin shaped like a rose, set with tiny red stones that matched the stones in her earrings, gleamed on her collar. Her mother's black dress would've looked plain and somber next to Mrs. Payson's party clothes.

Cleo wore the dress her grandmother made for the tea party. She, too, was wearing a flower pin, shaped like a violet and set with small, lavender stones. Matching violet earrings sparkled when she turned her head.

"Do you like them?" Cleo said, touching her ears to trace the outline of the flowers. "Daddy gave Granny and me presents tonight."

"They're beautiful," Molly answered. "Is it a holiday I don't know about?"

Mrs. Payson laughed. "Sugar, Cleo's daddy invents holidays. He says folks shouldn't need a reason to celebrate, we ought to just do it. William's so glad we're all coming tonight he went out and bought this jewelry, the first pin and earrings I've ever owned. Cleo, too. With the money he's making at the mill sometimes he can't resist acting like a rich man."

Cleo's grandmother shook her head. "This jewelry makes me feel so grand, like society folks. Sure enough, I might wear it to Mrs. Gable's house next week when I do her cleaning. That lady's mouth would pop open and she'd about jump out of her skin." She chuckled. "I'd like to see that."

"We're at the club, Granny," Cleo said, as the carriage slowed down. "There's Miss Cather with her friend, waiting for us."

Her grandmother paid the driver and they got out in front of a nondescript brick building with a small sign, "Southern Club", on its thick wooden door. Voices and laughter drifted out each time the door was opened. That happened often as people, after curious, sidelong glances at Miss Cather and Mr. Nevin, entered the club.

When Cleo introduced her grandmother to the pair, Miss Cather nodded, but the ebullient Ethelbert Nevin grabbed her hand and squeezed it.

"My dear Mrs. Payson, I can't tell you how pleased I am to be included. I've always admired ragtime as an art form. Musicians I knew in Italy talked about it; they say it's a truly American contribution to music. I do believe they're right."

"Reckon I don't know about that," she said, "but I've been listening to colored folks' music all my life and to me it sounds good—easy and natural, like tapping your foot. My son and his musician friends know their stuff. People always turn up to hear him play ragtime, but with his shifts at the mill he can't perform much. Let's go inside. They've saved us a table up front."

Molly and Cleo followed the others through a large room where tables were packed together, filling the floor space. The interior was dark and smoky; it took a while before Molly's eyes accommodated to the dim light. Men and women crowded around the tables and there was a hum of conversation. Glasses, food, and heavy ashtrays covered table surfaces. The smell of cigarettes mingled with perfume and food aromas.

As their group threaded its way among the tables to an empty one near the dance floor, Molly noticed pauses in conversation. People tried not to stare. Several waved to Mrs. Payson, then turned back to their companions; Molly knew they were startled to see white strangers. She remembered what Miss Bauman said about colored people needing their own clubs because they weren't welcome in white ones. If the situation were reversed, she wondered if white people would behave as courteously.

When they were seated a waiter approached, carrying a tray. "Lemonade for the young ladies and coffee for Mrs. Payson and her guests. Sandwiches for everyone."

Mr. Nevin reached into his pocket, but the waiter shook his head. "No sir. Compliments of Willie Payson. He'll soon be out to play."

Molly noticed Miss Cather looking around the room, studying the scene and the faces surrounding her.

She whispered to Cleo, sitting beside her. "Miss Cather's doing what she always tells us in class." She tried to imitate her teacher's intonation. "First, observe carefully, then describe and narrate clearly."

Cleo giggled. "I hope she's not taking notes."

Oblivious to the girls' whispers, Willa spoke to the adults. "In Nebraska I cherished landscape that rolled out like the sea. I've tried to get past my yearning for wide open spaces, but it's incurable. Yet, in this crowded room, there's a sense of openness and energy. People seem connected to each other, to this environment and this city. It's hard to explain."

Nevin nodded. "I feel it, too. I expect we'll hear it in the music."

They didn't have long to wait. William Payson moved quickly into the cleared place near their table, while the audience applauded and cheered. A small-boned, muscular man with the easy grace Molly admired in his daughter, he grinned at the crowd and bent his compact body into a deep bow.

Then he looked at the table where Cleo, her grandmother, and the others waited, winked and blew a kiss before he sat down at the piano. Dressed in a dark suit with a red satin vest and high-collared white shirt, he looked very dapper. Cleo sat up straight and glanced at Molly, eyes shining.

Never before had Molly heard the kinds of sounds he coaxed from the piano. Cleo had said her father admired a man named Scott Joplin, who'd come to Alabama to perform. Mr. Payson hitchhiked into town to hear him play and couldn't stop talking about it. Cleo's granny told them how her son used to hang around after Sunday services to play the church piano. At first, the minister shooed him out, but soon stayed to listen.

Molly understood why people liked listening to Mr. Payson's music. His fingers swept across the keys, making magical trills and rhythms, sounds that flew and plunged, floating on the air. Some of the notes repeated, then raced and soared before returning to patterns she'd heard earlier. Without intention, she was tapping her feet. Beside her, Cleo's head bobbed to the music.

When Willie Payson finished there was a roar from the crowd. People stood to applaud and cheer, Mr. Nevin among the first. Molly didn't understand his words to Miss Cather about neo-classical composition, unity of form, and harmony. The whole time, he was clapping so hard she wondered if his palms hurt.

Mr. Payson walked around the room, shaking hands and talking with friends. At their table, he kissed Cleo, his mother, and Molly, then shook hands with the others.

"My dear fellow," said Mr. Nevin, pumping his hand, "that was marvelous. What a privilege to have heard you. The symmetry, the sophistication of your style!"

The musician smiled. "That's too fancy for me. I just like to play."

"And you do that superbly," Miss Cather added, with the broad, bright smile she bestowed on the best of her students. "No wonder Cleo's so proud of you."

"I'm the proud one. This girl of mine's going to be important, a success in the world. She'll take care of her granny and me in our old age, won't you, baby?"

"Daddy, you're embarrassing me," Cleo said, but Molly knew she didn't really mind.

Too soon, Mrs. Payson said, "Time you girls got home. If you'll excuse us, we'll say good night."

They'd hoped to stay and hear more ragtime, but Cleo said there was no arguing with her grandmother. Their teacher and her friend were still talking with Mr. Payson as they prepared to leave.

"I'd be honored if you'd come out to my house and play. My friends would be thrilled to hear you and perhaps you could teach me more about ragtime," the composer said.

Molly didn't hear his answer. As they left Mrs. Payson kept stopping at tables to say hello and thank people for the compliments they paid her son. There were hugs for her and Cleo, who couldn't stop smiling.

For days afterward Molly talked about her evening at the club; Hannah, nodding, barely listened. She was probably distracted because of Simon's marriage and her sadness at not being there, so Molly forgave her. When her mother neglected some of her Settlement House visits, Molly's anxiety grew. Finally, she could stand it no longer.

"Mama, you must stop this worrying. Simon and his wife'll be fine and happy and Papa will write all the details of the trip to Minsk. Miss Bauman must be disappointed that you're missing classes."

Hannah sat down on the bed and looked at her daughter. They'd just returned from dinner downstairs and Molly noticed that her mother ate very little. She'd picked at her food, pushing it around on her plate, her mind clearly elsewhere.

"It's not the wedding. I'm getting used to the idea of not being there." She looked at Molly. "Well, almost. It's something else."

She twisted her hands in her lap, needing to explain in her own way. "You know Uncle Abe's been good to us, bringing us here and paying me to work in the store." She stopped and looked down at her clenched hands.

Molly waited, starting to worry herself.

"Lately, he's been saying he's getting old and wants to slow down, take it easy. Bella—Mrs. Bloom—is always telling him he shouldn't work so hard, he could have a nice, relaxed life if he wanted."

A tiny smile began at the corners of Hannah's mouth. "She wants to get married and she makes no secret of it. Who can blame Abe for thinking about it? She's a good person, trying to get him to have more pleasure in his life. Go see people, get out more. When she comes back from visiting her relatives in New York she tells him what an exciting place it is and how, if he wasn't working, he could go, too."

Hannah sighed, gloomy again. "Bella keeps repeating that he works too hard, he should sell the store so he can enjoy life. He used to laugh and say Bella was working overtime herself, as her own matchmaker. Now, the way he talks, he's getting to like the idea. When Bella's husband died he left her some money. She wants Abe to move from the rooms over the store so they can buy a nice house together. Maybe even live in New York."

Molly now understood her mother's fears. If Uncle Abe moved away, her strongest connection to America would be gone. And there was a bigger worry: if he gave up the store, Hannah would have no wages to pay the rent, or anything else. Papa didn't send money—the little he had was put aside to buy passage for him and David.

Molly looked at her mother, who seemed to be getting frailer instead of stronger in America. Her skin was like thin white paper; there were dark circles beneath her eyes. Her small hands, with long, tapered fingers, trembled in her lap. What if her mother was getting sick? People in their village who looked pale like Mamma began to cough and developed fever. Sometimes, when they coughed, blood came out. "Consumption" the neighbors whispered and the people were taken away to hospitals called sanitariums. More than a few of them never came back. Molly mustn't let that happen. She had to do better, try harder to keep her mother from worrying herself sick. What would she do if something happened to her mother? She couldn't bear to think about it. "Even if they marry, Mama, the store will be here and you'll still work in it."

Hannah shook her head. "I'm not so good at selling, Abe knows that. Sometimes I'm slow to understand what customers want. If the store is sold, the new owner would choose someone better. Or, if Abe decides to keep it and hire a manager, he won't need me. I have to find another job."

Molly went to her mother and put her arms around her. "You can do that. Think of everything you've learned since we came from Swidnik. And, when Papa and David come, you'll stay home and take care of the rest of us."

"Maybe, but now I have to work. I talked to Mrs. Torski, you know, who lives upstairs? She makes stogies and says I could get work doing that. They always need help and they hire greenhorns."

"You're not a greenhorn. You know English and you're getting very Americanized. You even know words I don't. What's a stogie?" Molly was glad to see the beginning of a smile.

"So, now you're the greenhorn. It's like a big cigarette, but smells stronger."

"A cigar? I didn't know they were called stogies."

"They make them here in the neighborhood," her mother explained. "Mrs. Torski says the women roll them. They work at a big table, with some kind of machine in front of them to finish the stogies. She says it's not hard, but your hands get tired and sometimes your back hurts from the way you sit all day. It's steady work, though, and the bosses aren't bad."

"It sounds terrible to me," Molly said. Then she was silent, thinking. "You know Victor Morelli quit school to work but he goes to classes at the Settlement House at night. I could do that, and get a job during the day."

She saw her mother's expression and added, "It would only be until Papa comes. Then I'd go back to regular school."

"Never," Mrs. Klein shouted. "I'd scrub floors first. You will finish high school and study some more after that, so you can be educated like Miss Bauman or that teacher you like so much."

"Miss Cather," Molly said. "She did go to college, in Nebraska, and Miss Bauman trained to be a nurse." Forgetting her earlier concerns, Molly talked about her own future. "I used to believe I wanted to teach like Miss Cather but lately I've thought about becoming a social worker like Miss Bauman. She does so many interesting, different things and if I help out at the Settlement House I can see if I really like the work."

Then Molly remembered the point of the original discussion. "You should talk to her about a job if Uncle Abe gives up the store. She'll have ideas that are a lot better than rolling stogies. Will you?"

"I already decided to speak to her."

"See how smart you are?" Molly said.

"You better do your schoolwork now or you won't feel so smart yourself tomorrow. I'll write to Papa and David about your visit to Mr. Payson's club and how you heard and liked the cloth music."

Molly stared at her, baffled, until realization struck. "Not cloth music—ragtime! Maybe you are a greenhorn, but Papa and David wouldn't know the difference."

Three days later Molly and her classmates were working at a writing assignment when they were interrupted by a knock at the door. Miss Cather answered, stepping into the corridor. When she returned she said, "Cleo, please come with me."

Cleo looked at Molly, made a comically questioning face, and left. After what seemed a long time, Miss Cather, pale and solemn, returned alone to the classroom. Soon, the bell to change classes rang.

"Please leave your papers on my desk. Molly, wait—I need to see you."

When the others had gone, Miss Cather spoke, so softly Molly could hardly hear her. "What I'm about to tell you is hard, but it's best you hear this terrible news from me."

Molly's heart thumped. Before she could consider what this was about, her teacher took her hand, held it tightly, and continued. "There's been an accident at the mill where Cleo's father works." Her voice quavered and Molly could see tears forming at the corners of her eyes. "Someone's come to take Cleo home. She doesn't know this yet, but Mr. Payson is dead."

Molly couldn't speak. She felt as if all the air was squeezed from her body. Her legs wobbled and she grabbed at a desk to keep from falling. Miss Cather steadied her and led her to a chair.

"Sit down and take deep breaths. That's it. Slowly."

When Molly stopped shaking her teacher pulled up another chair and sat beside her. "I know this is awful for you, but we have to think about Cleo now and what can be done to help her. She'll need you, Molly."

Molly nodded numbly. She couldn't trust herself to speak. In her mind, the same scene replayed: Mr. Payson, bent over the piano at the Southern Club, his fingers flying across the keys, face intent on the music; then, looking up to wink at Cleo, who sat beside her, eyes bright with love and pride. She must've been crying because Miss Cather handed her a white handkerchief, as crisp as the blouse she wore. Molly rubbed at her face and the cloth came away wet.

"We'll go to the Paysons now. I'll tell the principal we're leaving."

Molly sat motionless in the silent room, the crumpled handkerchief in her hand. Unthinking, she smiled at the notion of telling Cleo how she'd blown her nose in their teacher's fancy hanky. Then she remembered and tears started again.

When Miss Cather returned she was wearing a coat and a small, black hat. "Compose yourself now, Molly. Our job is to comfort Cleo and her grandmother. Get your coat and meet me in front of the building."

Molly nodded. Walking along the corridor, she passed a blur of classmates but didn't speak to anyone. If the others didn't know, they would soon enough, and she didn't want to be the one to tell. Besides, she couldn't trust herself to speak.

Outside, the air was chilly, despite the sun. When the wind blew, bits of grit from the smoke stacks stung Molly's face. Miss Cather took her arm and they hurried along, heads down to avoid the wind, occasionally dodging others doing the same.

As they neared the boarding house they heard the shrill call of a newspaper boy with a thick stack of *Pittsburgh Gazettes* tucked under his arm. He held one up to tempt passersby.

"Get your paper here. Read all about the accident at the mill. Three workers scalded to death. Read all about it."

In heavy black letters the headline read, "Boiler Blows to Pieces." Underneath, in letters nearly as big, "Grim Death for Mill Workers."

"Stay here," Willa Cather, her voice icy, said to Molly. "I'll be back soon."

Molly waited as her teacher approached the paperboy. She couldn't hear what was said, but she saw his expression change from defiance to solemn acceptance. He turned away from the block of boarding houses.

Molly, without thinking about it, slipped her hand into her teacher's and they climbed the stairs to the Paysons' rooms.

THIRTEEN

Inside, people filled the small rooms. Bowls and platters of food crowded Mrs. Payson's sewing table. Molly saw salads, cakes, bread, containers of soup. Near the table, Mrs. Payson sat with a man in a black suit and shirt with a high, stiff white collar. His hair was peppered with gray, his face shiny, darker than Mrs. Payson's and lined with wrinkles. He looked kind, Molly thought, and very sad.

"That must be the family's minister," Miss Cather whispered. "I'll speak to Mrs. Payson while you find Cleo."

Molly looked around the room. There were so many visitors standing together and talking in murmurs the familiar place was momentarily strange and confusing. Then she saw Cleo in a corner, surrounded by women who all seemed to be talking to her. At the same moment, Cleo saw her friend and, with a little cry, separated from the group and came toward her. Molly held out her arms and the two embraced. Cleo's thin shoulders shook as her sobs broke through. Finding no words of comfort, Molly could only hold her, her own tears flowing.

When Cleo's sobs subsided she whispered, "All these people talking at me is too much. Let's go outside."

The girls made their way past the visitors and out to the hall, where they sat on the steps of the landing. Cleo was trembling; Molly slipped out of her coat and draped it over Cleo's shoulders.

"I don't know if I want to talk about it," Cleo said, wiping her eyes.

"You don't need to. I'll just sit here with you."

She reached into her pocket for a handkerchief to give to Cleo. Her fingers found the limp cloth, rolled into a soggy ball.

"Miss Cather gave me this to use. It was folded into a triangle, with all the corners matching, and I've made it a mess. She'll have to throw it away."

Cleo looked at the sodden cloth bunched in her friend's hand. "Now you're probably gonna' flunk English."

"Then you'll have to take it over, too, so we can be in the same class."

Cleo shook her head, returning to the present and her grief. "I don't think we'll be together."

Watching her, Molly waited for more, but Cleo muttered, "I don't want to talk about it. Don't want to talk at all."

Molly, arm around her friend, sat beside her as Cleo wept, only her soft sobs breaking the silence.

She didn't know how long they stayed there, people passing them on the stairs and stopping to pat Cleo's shoulder or, eyes reflecting their pain, shake their heads and move on. It was Miss Cather's voice that broke the silence.

"I must leave now, but I'll be back." She took Cleo's hands and drew her up, looking hard into her eyes. Molly stood, too. "My dear," she said. "You must always remember your father's pride in naming you Cleopatra, after a strong and beautiful woman who was a leader in the world. That was his dream for you and he knew you'd live up to your name. I believe you will."

Cleo looked at her teacher and nodded.

"I'm going now, to find Miss Bauman at the Settlement House. You remember her, Cleo, from the tea party?"

Cleo nodded again and Miss Cather continued, still holding her hands. "She knows practical, useful ways to help families through trouble. Please listen to her and allow her to help you and your grandmother."

"I will," Cleo said.

"Good," Miss Cather answered and released her hands. "Molly, will you be staying?"

"Yes, ma'am. As long as Cleo wants me to."

"Good," she said and turned away.

"We better go back inside. Granny will be wondering about me," Cleo said.

In the apartment, Molly stayed near Cleo as people came up to speak to her. Finally, most of them left and the room grew quieter. Mrs. Payson remained where she'd been, the man in the black suit and white collar by her side.

"Molly, sugar, come over and say hello to the Reverend Simms," Mrs. Payson called to her. "He's been asking about the girl who's been with my Cleo all day. I told him you're her best friend, the two of you always together."

Molly went to the man, who took her hand in his big, warm grasp.

"I recollect seeing you now, in the neighborhood. Don't you work in Mr. Klein's chicken store?"

"Yes sir. He's my uncle. My mother works there and when she has to be away, I fill in for her."

"Of course," he said. "I know her, a quiet, sweet lady who works hard. And your uncle, with the big voice and even bigger cigar." He smiled. "A good man. Always a joke for me when I come in. Calls me "Rev" and likes to tease, but he's honest and fair with all his customers. He ever goin' to marry that widow lady who keeps bringing him food and new neckties?"

"She hopes so," Molly answered, pleased to see Cleo smile.

"I can tell you chicken store folks are related—same kind of humor. Does your daddy work there, too? I don't believe I've met him."

"He's still in Poland, where we lived before. All of us couldn't leave, so Papa sent Mama and me when Uncle Abe offered to help us. We hope my father and brother, David, will come soon. My other brother just married a Russian girl, so he'll be living there. Mama worries all the time that Papa and David won't be allowed to leave Poland. The government there has hard rules about Jewish people and sometimes won't let them leave without paying bribes. Papa can't afford much. I'm scared Mama's making herself sick, she's so pale and she's always tired. I can't make her feel better, no matter how hard I try."

Molly stopped, surprised at blurting out so much to someone she didn't know. It was his eyes, she thought, so kind as they looked at her, encouraging her to say what she usually kept inside. "Sometimes, I feel bad because I like it here, and Mama's so unhappy. I want us to be Americans but all she thinks about is Swidnik."

Reverend Simms shook his head, his brown eyes still studying her. "We get so caught up in our own troubles we forget our neighbors carry heavy burdens, too. When does your mama think your daddy's coming?"

"We don't know. He has to find someone to take over his tailor shop, wait for papers from the government, and find passage on a ship for him and David. My father needs to have enough money to pay for all the papers and the boat, too. And extra to pay off the people in charge. Mama cries when she thinks about it."

"I'll pray for them, child, and say so to your mother the next time I see her."

There was a soft knock at the door and Miss Bauman, Victor Morelli behind her, looked in. "I hope it's all right that I'm here, Mrs. Payson. Cleo's teacher came to the Settlement House to tell me. Victor was there for a class and asked to come, too. Hello, Reverend Simms," she said, extending her hand.

He took her hand and held it. "I'm mighty glad you're here. Do you know the Paysons?"

"I met Cleo at a tea party."

Mr. Simms raised his eyebrows. "Do tell! I didn't know this little lady was getting around in Pittsburgh society."

Miss Bauman stepped close and spoke to Mrs. Payson. "I'm so sorry for your loss. I came hoping I could help you with some of the arrangements you'll need to make. My work at the Settlement House has, unfortunately, given me a good deal of experience in these matters."

Before Cleo's grandmother could respond, Mr. Simms said, "I'll be leaving you for a while then, Jenny, knowing you're in good hands. Let Miss Bauman help, the way she's done for lots of folks here on the Hill." He said goodbye to Victor and Molly and hugged Cleo. "You take good care of your Granny and yourself, hear?" Then he left, quietly closing the door behind him.

Victor sat down beside Cleo and put his arm around her. "Sorry I wasn't here sooner, but I went straight to class after I cleaned up from work, so I didn't know. Anything I can do for you?"

She shook her head. "I'm just glad you're here. I've missed you."

"Me, too. Working every day and going to school at night doesn't leave much time for friends."

Molly said, "It won't be too long until school vacation for Christmas. Maybe we can get together then."

"We could go back to the ice cream parlor," Victor said. "Or how about going to see a play on the stage at the Newcomb? My treat. I'm making good money working with my father and uncles. In the spring we'll be moving to a house in East Liberty, with three bedrooms, so Uncle Gino won't have to sleep on the front room couch much longer. You two can come out on the streetcar to visit and Mama'll cook a big spaghetti dinner."

Molly noticed that Cleo didn't respond. Not only the shock and the sadness, but something else was gnawing at her friend, too. She was certain of it.

With the other visitors gone, Molly couldn't help hearing the conversation between Miss Bauman and Mrs. Payson in the quiet room.

"We can take care of the details," the social worker was saying. "Arrangements for the burial, whatever needs to be done. Settlement House gets funds from benefactors for family emergencies. Just tell me what you want done and I'll start the process."

"You don't understand," Mrs. Payson said, speaking as if getting the words out hurt her mouth. "Cleo and I won't be burying my boy here. We're going home."

Molly's head snapped up and she looked at her friend. Cleo avoided meeting her eyes.

"Mr. Powers, down at the funeral home, will get William's body—what's left of it, God help us—and when that's done we'll get on a train to go back where we came from, Alabama. My boy had a big dream, you know—" Her voice cracked; she rubbed a hand across her eyes and continued. "He was going to build us a fine life up here. Get his baby a good education, make lots of money to buy a piano and a nice house to put it in. He'd get that twinkle in his eye and say maybe he'd play his music in other cities, travel around the country and perform for folks who love ragtime. Yessir, that boy was always planning, hoping and dreaming."

Cleo went to her grandmother, sat beside her and held her hand.

"Funny what happens to dreams. You put body and soul into making them come true, like my William. You give the people you love what you think will make them happy—pretty things to wear to church. And, all the time, the big, important men who own the factories don't care about folks like my boy. Don't matter to them if the workers are safe around those hellfires in the mill. All they care about is their almighty dollars. Do they feel a minute's grief that my son died in agony? That he was boiled alive! Didn't matter to them when men called William a lazy nigger. They didn't praise him when he worked harder and better to show the negro haters they were wrong. The bosses didn't pay any mind to the shaming he took every day he went to work. And they had the nerve to send flowers! Flowers and a note saying how sorry they were. The flowers and the lying words went in the garbage with the other trash." Choking off tears, Mrs. Payson reached for Cleo and pulled her close.

Miss Bauman spoke softly. "He wanted to make a happy life for you and Cleo. People with dreams, like William, make this world a better place. He did succeed, you know—think of all the folks who loved his music, and of Cleo's outstanding grades at school. You have so much to be proud of and later, when things feel more normal, and Cleo's back at school with Molly and her other friends—"

"No!" Mrs. Payson's answer sounded loud, harsh and unnatural in the quiet room. "This is no place for my grandchild and me. The city killed my boy, filling his head with ideas and yearnings that never could happen. He dreamed too much, so he put up with all the ugliness from men who don't want our kind here. And he wore himself down, always needing to prove those evil people calling him names and trying to make him quit were wrong.

"William took too many chances, putting himself in danger so they couldn't say he was lazy or too stupid to do his job. Nobody but me knows how many times he came home downhearted, too worn out to think, let alone play his music."

"Mrs. Payson," Miss Bauman interrupted, "Maybe you should rest, lie down for a while . . ."

"No, let me finish. My son was a good man. Too good to die in agony because some machine that should've been fixed, wasn't. The bosses didn't pay no mind about safety, so the boiler blew up. William and the others didn't stand a chance." Tears rolled down her face, but she ignored them. "Steam scorched them like they were nothing but pigs for roasting." She swiped at the tears rolling down her face. "Maybe we'll never have much fancy stuff back home, but Cleo will be among folks who care about her, breathing air that's clean, and looking at blue sky. We'll leave for home in a few days, soon as arrangements for the trip are completed."

"What about school, Mrs. Payson? Cleo's an excellent student, with opportunities here to continue her education. That's what her father wanted. What chances will she have in a colored school in your little town in Alabama?"

Miss Bauman's question echoed in Molly's head—that, and how she could get along without her best friend. If only Miss Bauman could make Cleo's grandmother change her mind! When Molly looked at Mrs. Payson's set jaw and tight face she knew that wouldn't happen.

"I hear you and you're right that my William's biggest dreams were for Cleo's future. But I have to do what's in my heart. The good Lord'll make it come out all right. Now, if y'all will excuse us, I'm weary, so I'll say good night for this child and me."

When Molly embraced Cleo, her friend stood stiff and unyielding. "I'll come to see you tomorrow after school," she said. Cleo's only answer was a shrug.

Walking down the stairs from the Paysons' rooms, Molly could barely see for the tears. She sat on the steps of her own boarding house, shoulders heaving and stomach muscles aching from sobs she didn't try to control. The world could be a terrible place when a man like Mr. Payson died in unimaginable pain.

And her own father—would she ever see him again? If not, that would kill her mother. Hannah, sickly and frail, could not survive without her husband; she would never be happy in America without him and David.

The wave of sadness engulfed her. How could Cleo, who adored her father, learn to live without him? Molly missed her own father, had always believed his absence was temporary—but what if it wasn't? She needed him, just as Cleo needed Mr. Payson.

Kind, gentle Papa, who always listened and understood her, even when she hardly understood herself. He would have known just what to say to Cleo, maybe even been able to persuade her grandmother to stay. Her brothers would know how to help her get through this sadness, but, most of all, she needed her father to comfort her.

Molly would write to him tonight and tell him about Cleo. She would tell him, too, how much she missed him. Then, like her mother, she would wait for his letter to her, reassuring her that all would be well.

And how can I get along without my best friend? Molly thought. She remembered how lonely and different she'd felt during the first year in Pittsburgh, with no one her own age to talk to. She didn't understand what her classmates were saying much of the time, and she was sure they were laughing at her. How odd she must have appeared, how pathetic a greenhorn.

Molly had hated going to school, forcing herself to leave the boarding house. She was ashamed of her clothes, her accent, even of her mother, who spoke no English and sold chickens. All that changed when she met Cleo and Victor. They wanted her to be their friend; they made her feel welcome. Because of them, especially Cleo, she began to like Pittsburgh. Now, she'd lost them both—Cleo was leaving and she rarely saw Victor. Without them, she felt like a greenhorn again, a stranger who could never be a real American.

The next days were bleak, like enduring a nightmare. Molly tried to concentrate on school, but the aching knowledge that

Cleo soon would be gone never left her. After school, when she went to the Paysons, her friend spoke in lifeless monosyllables.

On one visit, Molly could stand it no longer. "Cleo, this isn't right and you know it as well as I do. You have to make your grandmother change her mind. You're too smart to go to some awful little country school where they don't know you and won't appreciate you like we do here."

Her friend sat beside her, face expressionless, ignoring her words.

"If you won't say something, I will. I'm going to talk to your grandmother and tell her what a mistake she's making. Moving down South is not what your daddy would want for you."

Cleo reached out, grabbing her arm in a grip that made Molly wince. "Don't you dare. Who do you think you are, trying to tell Granny and me what to do? You don't know any more about what's in our hearts than you do about your own mother's."

Molly felt as if she'd been slapped. She knew Cleo was grieving, but how could she be so hurtful? Didn't their friendship mean anything after all? She got up to leave, saying nothing to Cleo and only a subdued goodbye to Mrs. Payson. Cleo stayed seated, ignoring her.

On her last visit to the Paysons' rooms, this time with her mother, whose gift of a sponge cake baked in Uncle Abe's kitchen used a week's supply of eggs, Molly had given up even trying to talk to her friend. Mrs. Payson was polite and friendly, but Cleo barely responded. Her silence hurt, a painful reminder to Molly of the times when they never ran out of things to say to each other.

In the late afternoon, two days later, Molly was preparing an English assignment when she heard a knock at the door. "Cleo!" she shouted when she opened it. "Am I glad to see you!"

"Are you busy?" Cleo asked, sitting on the edge of the bed near the table where Molly's papers were spread.

"Homework for Miss Cather."

"Let me guess. You have to write about three poems, identify and explain similes and metaphors, analyze themes, and be ready to recite two from memory for class tomorrow."

Molly smiled. That sounded like the old Cleo. "Not exactly, but you have her idea of a simple assignment right. This time it's about *Huckleberry Finn*. Miss Cather said that although Mark Twain sometimes 'behaved like a provincial clown and all-around tough'"—Molly mimicked her tone—"she 'admires his novel'. You'd like the funny parts, Cleo, and the boys' adventures."

"Maybe I'll try to read it when we get settled. We leave tomorrow, so I came to say goodbye." After an awkward pause, she hurried on. "Miss Bauman helped us a lot. She made arrangements for the train and for shipping—the coffin. She got the bosses at the mill to pay for everything. When Granny fussed, Miss Bauman just worked around her." Cleo smiled. "She's the only person I ever did meet who's as hard-headed as my granny." She stopped, looked at Molly, then said, "There's something I want to give you." Cleo reached in her pocket and retrieved a small package, handing it to Molly.

A cry escaped from Molly's lips when she opened it. "It's the violet pin you wore to the club. I can't take this."

Cleo pressed her hand around Molly's so their fingers closed around the gift. "I want you to have it so you'll always remember that night and how good a musician my daddy was."

"I don't need this to remember. The pin was his special gift to you."

"It's all right. I have the earrings and when I wear them, knowing you're wearing the matching pin, it'll be almost like we're together. You're the best friend I ever had. You and Victor were my second family here."

Before Molly, eyes brimming with tears, could answer, Cleo stood. "I didn't say goodbye to Victor." An impish look teased at the corners of her mouth. "Tell him I said Vittorio; that'll get him. Will you do it for me?"

Molly nodded, not trusting herself to speak.

"You'll be a great social worker, Molly. You're almost as stubborn as Miss Bauman and you like to take care of people. Tell Miss Cather I'll miss her class. Maybe I'll write to you when we get settled down home—unless it makes me too sad." Cleo hugged her and was gone before Molly could say anything.

FOURTEEN

In the weeks after Cleo left Molly went through the motions of living her life. She did her homework, helped in the store, and listened when her mother wanted to practice new words. If Miss Cather stopped her after class to ask how she was getting along, Molly answered, "Fine."

Her teacher frowned, waiting for a more complete and honest response, but Molly had nothing to say. Instead, she made some excuse about being late for her next class. She knew Miss Cather wanted to help, but there was nothing she could do. Cleo was gone and she had to learn to get along without her.

One damp, cold winter afternoon Molly hurried away from Central. Head down and shoulders hunched against the wind, she nearly collided with Victor Morelli. He reached out to steady her, grinning.

"I was waiting here, hoping to bump into you, but I didn't expect it to happen so literally."

"Literally?" Her brow furrowed. "Is that word English or Italian?"

It was Victor's turn to look puzzled. "You're joking, right?"

Molly chuckled, realizing it'd been a long time since anything struck her as funny. "Yes, but I still don't know what it means," she said as he fell into step beside her.

After he'd explained, he said, "If I keep learning so much at the Settlement House you'll need a dictionary just to talk to me."

"Oh, yeah! This is your *paesano*, remember?"

"So you're going to speak to me in Italian? I guess that's what happens when I have to teach you English. Are you going to your uncle's store?"

"Not for a while. My mother's there; I'll go later when she has to leave for her class. I was heading home to study—big math assignment and I don't understand half of it."

"How's this for a plan? Come with me now and I'll help you with your math homework."

"Where? And why aren't you working?" Molly said.

"The weather's so bad my uncles decided to quit early. That's okay with me, because I can get to my classes sooner. By spring I'll be caught up with the regular school. Then, Mr. Brownell says, we'll move into more advanced work, and if I can squeeze in the rest of the required stuff I'll probably be able to graduate when you do, with our class."

"Maybe you can be in the commencement ceremony with the rest of us," Molly said.

"I don't care about that, but it'd make my mother happy."

"You still haven't told me where we're going."

"Settlement House," Victor said, "to see Miss Bauman."

"What about?"

"I don't know exactly, but she said she'd like to talk to you."

"About my mother?" Molly said, sounding worried. "I hope nothing's wrong."

"I doubt it." Victor looked at Molly. "Is something the matter with your mother?"

"She isn't sick, if that's what you mean, but she's worried about what'll happen if Uncle Abe gets married. I haven't paid much attention and she knows I've been upset about Cleo, so she hasn't said much."

A sleety rain began to fall, stinging their faces.

"When winter comes I always wish my family'd gone to Mexico when they left Italy," Victor grumbled. "Good thing that's the Settlement House up ahead or we'd turn into ice statues."

"Not you. You wave your arms around when you talk and move too fast to freeze."

He laughed. "If I was in Mexico I'd move slower and lie in the sun all day."

"Your uncles wouldn't let you," she answered.

"You're right. They'd probably put me to work paving the beach."

He held the door open for her and they hurried inside, grateful for the blast of warm air.

"Why should your mother care if your uncle gets married?" Victor said. "Doesn't she like the bride-to-be?"

"It's hard to think of Bella Bloom as a bride, but, no, that's not it. She's all right, even though she invites us to dinner and stuffs me so full of food I can hardly move. If we don't take second helpings of everything her feelings are hurt, so before we go my uncle always tells me I have to ask for more. When we finally leave her house I feel like one of those geese Miss Cather talked about. Remember, the ones they force-feed to make their livers big so rich people can put a fancy spread on their crackers."

"Bella and my mama would get along fine, but you're straying from the subject," Victor said.

"Right. If Uncle Abe marries her, Bella wants him to stop working, give up the store so they can have time to enjoy themselves. Mama's afraid she won't have a job, so she's thinking about other work, like making cigars."

"I can't imagine your uncle just sitting around, letting Bella fatten him up like that goose you were talking about."

Molly smiled. "Maybe they'll travel to Mexico and sit in the sun. You can visit and pave a place on the beach for them."

"Only if Bella will feed me. Why don't you go see Miss Bauman now and then I'll meet you in that first room down the hall from her office. There's a desk and chairs in there and we can work on your math assignment."

Molly nodded and went looking for Miss Bauman. Nearing her office, Molly saw that the door was open; the social worker was speaking with a younger woman. Small and very slender, her dark hair wound around her head in a heavy braid, the visitor was apparently discussing something important, her tone low and insistent.

Molly started to turn away, when Miss Bauman saw her.

"I'll be back when you're not busy," she said.

"Come in, Molly. Your arrival couldn't be more timely. I'd like you to meet Maria Brennan. She's in charge of children's programs and she's been telling me how desperate she is for help. This is Molly Klein. Her mother Hannah's often here and has shown so much progress she may soon be in our employment training program." Miss Bauman smiled at Molly. "I haven't told her about that yet, but it should ease her concerns about losing her job."

Molly must have looked surprised because Miss Bauman answered her unasked question. "Hannah told me about it, but we'll discuss that another time. Now, I'd like you to think about helping Maria with the little children. We won't be able to pay you, but it's good training for your career. Hannah says you're considering social work."

"I think so, but I'm not sure. I still have to finish high school."

"All the more reason to work with us and see how you like it," Miss Bauman answered.

"You'd enjoy the children," Maria said. "They're affectionate and responsive to attention. If you help after school you'll get to teach them and play with them."

"How many children are in the group?" Molly said. The question popped out of her mouth while thoughts scurried like insects in her head. Could she do this? What if the children didn't like her or ignored her because she wasn't trained to work with them? Would Uncle Abe object to her taking time away from the store? She tried to focus on what Maria was saying.

"It depends. If the mothers work and have no one to look after their children, they bring them here. Mostly, the families are immigrants with no relatives to help them. The parents like to bring the children here even when they're not working because we read to them and teach language through games. The adults don't understand much English, but they know they want better lives for their kids."

Maria continued, her large brown eyes intent on Molly. "They have very little and the wives are always looking for ways to add to their husbands' earnings. They take in laundry, work odd shifts in the stogie factories, do housework for wealthier Pittsburghers. Things like that, so the children are often with us all day. We try to provide nutritious food for them."

Molly wondered why this woman was telling her things about immigrants she knew only too well. The families described weren't that different from her own. Without Uncle Abe's help, they'd be in the same situation.

As if reading her mind, Miss Bauman said, "Molly's familiar with the problems of these families. She and her mother came from Poland four years ago. Her father and brother are still there."

"Of course. Stupid of me. I should've known when you mentioned her mother coming here. It's just that you seem so . . ." She broke off, embarrassed.

"American?" Miss Bauman finished for her. "It's true, Molly. You've lost your accent, so someone who doesn't know you would assume you were born here."

For some time now, Molly hadn't paid much attention to the way she spoke, probably because it felt natural. Except for her family, she rarely thought about Poland. She hardly remembered the friends she'd had there. Her house and the town where she was born were fading from her memory.

"I do feel at home here. More than my mother does," Molly said, the familiar guilt over her impatience with Mama returning.

"Hannah will be better when Nathan and David arrive. Let's hope it won't be much longer. Now, go along with Maria and let her show you how to help us."

Molly walked with Maria to a part of the building she hadn't seen before. In a large room painted vivid yellow to offset its institutional look, three groups of children sat on low wooden chairs, forming a circle around an adult.

At the center of the first circle a woman pointed to a picture in a book she held up, said a word, and waited while the children repeated it with varying degrees of success. In another group a girl not much older than Molly was reading a story, complete with animal sound effects that made the children giggle. The third circle played a game that included raising arms, kicking legs, and clapping.

Maria spoke softly as they watched. "We try to teach them words through games, stories, and pictures. Most catch on quickly, then go home and teach the words to their parents. We have milk for them, sometimes soup, and bread and butter. For special occasions, like holidays, families bring in cakes and cookies. Wealthier people in the city contribute food or money to buy supplies for the children."

One tiny girl, her long brown braids tied with red ribbons, left the game circle, came running to them, and threw her arms around Maria's knees.

"This is Katya," she said, tweaking a braid, then bending down to pick her up. "She's a special friend."

"Friend," Katya repeated and burrowed her head into Maria's neck. As she snuggled, Maria spoke to Molly, concern clear in her eyes.

"Katya's mother has been sick for several months and her father works a twelve-hour shift at the mill, so I've been stopping at their boarding house in the morning to get Katya and bring her here. We've tried to get the mother hospitalized, but so far no luck. Neighbors look in on her and one takes her to the clinic when she can, but it's not a good arrangement.

"The father can't take time off or he'll lose his job." She sighed. "I don't know what will happen, but Miss Bauman's working on it and she usually gets results. Meanwhile, Katya's happy here and that makes us feel better." She put the child down. "Go back to your group now, sweetheart. I'll see you later, after I show Molly what we do here."

Her bright eyes fastening on the newcomer, Katya said, "Molly," and ran back to her circle of children.

Molly smiled at Maria. "I know you didn't plan this, but if I wasn't sure before, Katya won me over. Tell me how I can help."

By the time Molly returned to the room where she was to meet Victor, she'd scheduled three days of after-school work at the Settlement House. She would help wherever she was needed—the learning circles, feeding the children and practicing English with them, and taking them home when their parents couldn't come for them. The only complication was arranging her volunteering so it wouldn't interfere with her work in her uncle's store.

The next day, when Molly talked to him about it, Uncle Abe was agreeable. "Sure, sure, kid, it'll be all right. They do good work there. I like that Miss Bauman, she has lots of spunk." He laughed. "Years ago, before you and your mother were here, she came to the store to argue about some lazy greenhorn who worked for me for a little while. He was terrible—wouldn't pick up a broom and insulted my customers—so I fired him."

Remembering, Abe scowled. "At the time, his wife was learning English at the Settlement House. She was nicer than him, smarter, too. So, this loafer tells his wife to complain to the Settlement House lady about how I fired him and she should get his job back. One busy Friday morning, in comes Miss Bauman to talk about that bum. I'm waiting on my customers and, in-between, she starts asking questions. Before I can answer, Mrs. Goodman—you know her, she's the nosy one—gives her an earful about the greenhorn and how he insulted her and three of her lady friends and called them dirty names in Lithuanian. I said, 'You're not Lithuanian, how do you know they were dirty?' She said she could tell by the way he said them."

Uncle Abe chuckled. "That's all Miss Bauman had to hear. She apologized for interrupting me at my business and it was the last I heard about that good-for-nothing."

No customers were in the store. Her uncle went to the back, pulled out a crate he liked to sit on, and lit up one of his fat, smelly cigars, a sign he was in a good mood. "So you're gonna' be a social worker, eh? That's good, your Papa will like his little girl helping people."

"I'm not a little girl. I'm in high school. Practically grown up. Mama was engaged to Papa when she was my age."

"That was the old country. Here, everything's different. Girls have a chance to be somebody, like boys." He blew a cloud of smoke. "Don't worry about not spending enough time in the store. I'm thinking of cutting back myself."

Molly resisted the urge to wrinkle her nose in disgust at the odor. "What do you mean?" she said.

"I'm not getting any younger, you know, and I need to relax more, take it easy. Bella and I have even been talking about marriage." He looked sideways at her, gauging her reaction. "Don't laugh at the idea of an old fool getting married."

"I'm not. Mrs. Bloom's a nice lady and you've been alone a long time. If that's what you want, I'm glad for you."

"It gets too lonely, being by yourself. If I get married we could live in her house—it has more room than my place above the store—or, maybe, find something bigger. Travel a little. Go visit old friends and her relatives in New York."

Molly was only half listening. Her uncle's apartment had always seemed grand to her. With two bedrooms, a front room, and a separate kitchen, it was a palace compared to the boarding house. "I'm surprised you'd give up your apartment," she said.

He shrugged. "Bella likes her place, furnished with things she bought with her husband. She has expensive taste, so it's lucky he had a good business, a fish store right down the street. She's going from fish to chicken. Coming up in the world!"

He blew another puff of smoke. "I know your Mama's concerned about all this. Not about Bella, but the business. She shouldn't worry. Hannah doesn't say much, just that I should do what's best for me, but I don't like her to be upset."

Molly nodded, but she understood her mother's anxiety. She'd tell her what Uncle Abe said. Maybe her talk about another job wasn't so unrealistic. Molly only hoped it didn't have to be in a stogie factory.

"Before you go, Malkele . . ."

Molly's heart felt like it was ready to jump out of her chest. Her uncle never called her by her pet Yiddish name. Was he softening her up to tell her something terrible? She didn't know if she could take any more bad news.

Her uncle's voice was quieter than usual, another worrisome sign. "I know sometimes I don't seem so nice to you and your Mama. Bella's always telling me I sound like I'm ready to bite your heads off, but I don't mean you should take it to heart. That's the way I am. Life kicks me, I'm always ready to kick back. But not at you and Hannah. It's just you're both—not you so much as your Mama—so soft in the way you see the world. You, it's all right, you're young and everything's ahead of you. But Hannah—well, I try to toughen her up, make her ready for life's hard knocks. So people won't take advantage of her sweet ways, you know?"

Molly nodded, too surprised by her uncle's words to respond.

Abe scratched his chin, hesitating while he decided how to continue. Then he smiled at Molly. "But, I'm sure you noticed, she doesn't let me change her. In her own quiet way she's as obstinate as you are and she just behaves like always, nice and friendly to everyone. I understand why your Papa is so proud of her—and of you. So when I'm yelling at you or your Mama, ignore me the way Bella does."

Her heart beating normally again, Molly went to her uncle and planted a kiss on his gristled cheek. He looked startled, but pleased, as he pulled away. "Enough with the mushy stuff. Go do what you're supposed to be doing."

"I bet you don't say that to Bella," Molly retorted as she left the store. When she looked back, her uncle was still grinning.

Although she missed Cleo every day—there was no one who could take her place——time passed quickly and the pain of losing her best friend receded. The hours at the Settlement House helped most. Each visit, Molly found something gratifying to do. She especially liked helping in the children's circles. Soon, she was reading stories and learning songs to teach them, amazed at how quickly they caught on. Preparing to leave one night, she mentioned this to Maria.

"Children learn languages more easily when they're young than at a later age. That's why we concentrate on English practice with the little ones. To them, it's a game. At home they easily shift back into the language they speak with their families, but our hope is they'll teach older relatives their new words."

Molly nodded. "I shouldn't be surprised, thinking about my own family. My father started us learning English in Poland. I suppose, because I was the youngest, I caught on quicker than my brothers. It used to make them really mad, especially my oldest brother."

"You must miss them. How long since you've seen them?"

"More than four years." She paused, thinking about it. "I don't miss my brothers as much as you'd think. Simon seemed much older, even when we were all together. Now he's married, living in Russia, and I can hardly imagine that. David and I were closer, but he always treated me like a baby. I don't know what he'd be like now. I was close to my father and lately I've been thinking about him a lot. My best friend lost her dad in a mill accident and It made me remember how important my own father has been in my life. I wrote to tell him that. I don't write often but my mother does, every week. She's so lonely for Papa and the others that I feel guilty for not sharing her sadness."

"You shouldn't," Maria said. "America's your home now. I'm sure your mother's happy with the way you fit in here."

"I hope. She tries not to cry when she talks about Simon. She knows she probably won't ever see him again or get to know his wife and the children they'll have."

"Unless they come to America, too. They might, you never know."

On the way back to the boarding house Molly thought about what Maria had said. It was true her roots were here now. But she wished things were better for her mother and that she could stop feeling bad about adding to Hannah's sadness by forgetting about Poland.

FIFTEEN

As winter closed in on the city, Molly was immersed in her busy schedule. Miss Cather and other teachers piled on homework. Like her classmates, she didn't dare complain; anyone who did was swiftly reprimanded. When Henry Grinnell groaned too loudly about a reading assignment, Miss Cather glared at him.

"With that attitude you'll not get far in this world, Grinnell," she'd said. "Only ambition and willingness to work hard lead to success. I, too, have assignments to complete, in addition to teaching. When an editor requests an article, it must be ready exactly when he wants it. If it's a review for an opera or a concert, no matter how much I'm enjoying it, I force myself to leave the theater early, go home and do my work, so that the story's finished on time. None of this Henry Grinnell nonsense." She breathed a deep, exaggerated sigh and made a face that mimicked Henry's frown. Everyone but Henry chuckled.

"Do you suppose I can tell the editor I have too many essays to correct and that a few, like Grinnell's, are so full of mistakes they take hours to mark? Of course not. We must all do our work and I want no more groans, muttering, or sour faces. Understood?"

"Yes, ma'am," Henry answered, so loudly that the other students laughed, Miss Cather joining them.

When she finished at school Molly hurried to the store or the Settlement House. She did her homework sitting on the wooden crate at the back of the store. Uncle Abe wasn't around much. Molly asked about him, but her mother said Abe wasn't required to tell them where he went. Molly guessed he was visiting Bella.

Hannah Klein was quieter, less inclined than usual to ask Molly about school and her work with Maria. There were fewer opportunities to talk. After supper at the boarding house, Molly usually did schoolwork while her mother worked at assignments from Miss Bauman. Often, Molly didn't get home from the Settlement House in time for the evening meal, eating with the children instead.

One frigid February night, as Molly prepared to leave the Settlement House, Maria stopped her. "Miss Bauman wants to see you in her office and if you hurry you can catch her before she gets involved with something else."

Molly detached herself from the group of clinging three-year-olds who'd become her special charges, grabbed her coat and mittens, and hurried down the hall to a chorus of shouts and goodbyes.

The Settlement House director was bent over a stack of papers, glasses perched on the end of her nose as she riffled through the pile. She looked up when Molly tapped on her open door. "Come in, my dear. I've been hoping for a chance to speak with you. Just move that clutter on the chair and sit down."

As Molly shifted the files and stacks of mail to the floor, Miss Bauman looked at her with a bemused smile. "Sometimes I think all this stuff secretly reproduces when I leave the room so I'm always wading through papers and never catch up. Maria tells me you're a wonderful help in the Children's Room."

"I hope so. I like working there."

"I thought you would. Maria says you have a gift for teaching the little ones. Hannah must be proud of what you're doing."

Molly avoided the other woman's eyes, looking down at the floor. "She doesn't say much. She's always thinking about Papa and the boys, but lately—well, I don't know what it is, but something's really worrying her."

Miss Bauman gave her a sharp look. "I've noticed that, too. It's why I wanted to talk to you."

"Maybe she's upset about what will happen if Uncle Abe gives up the store," Molly said.

"I don't think so. She has some ideas about training for other work. In fact, she was planning to begin a class in office skills: filing, typing, learning dictation. I've assured her she could do them and she was enthused about starting. But her teacher says she's missed the last three classes. That isn't like your mother."

Molly's stomach knotted. Maybe the illness she'd always feared had struck and she'd been too caught up in her own life to notice. She looked down at her coat folded on her lap, trying to collect her thoughts before meeting Miss Bauman's eyes again. "I can't explain it. I didn't even know she was studying office skills. How thoughtless can I get?"

"You mustn't blame yourself. Hannah understands how busy you are. Has she been working longer hours at the store so she's had to miss classes?"

Molly shook her head. "She usually asks me to help when she needs to come here. My uncle encourages her to learn, so I don't think that's the problem."

"Then I wish you'd find out what it is and let me know," Miss Bauman said. "I'll try to help."

Molly nodded, stood, and put on her coat. "Thank you for telling me." She said goodbye and started down the corridor, halted by a familiar voice.

"What luck! I was going to stop by your place on my way home." Victor fell into step beside her, looking cheerful. It had been a while since they were together. The good times with him and Cleo seemed distant, like half-remembered dreams.

"If you're leaving, I'll walk you home."

She nodded and waited as he buttoned his jacket and tugged open the heavy wooden door. They were met by a blast of wind and Molly pulled her coat collar up to shield her face. "When I was a little kid in Poland I hated weather like this. The mud streets would freeze into thick, hard lumps I kept tripping over."

They braced their shoulders as they walked into the wind. "It's easier here than in the old country. My *paesanos* paved the streets so you wouldn't fall on frozen mud," Victor said.

"Then I wish your *paesanos* would do something about the dirt from the mills that turns the snow all gray and ugly."

"We're working on it. How're you doing?"

She told him about her work with the children, about school and some of their classmates.

"Have you heard from Cleo?" Victor said.

Molly shook her head. "We didn't promise anything about writing and I don't expect to hear from her. I think Cleo decided, when her grandmother made her go back to Alabama, that she didn't want any reminders of her life here."

"Maybe she'll change her mind. I'm sure she misses you."

"I miss her, too. I was sad for a long time and it made me remember how I used to go to my father when something was bothering me. I wrote to him about Cleo and Mr. Payson, but no answer yet. I haven't had much time to think about him or Cleo, or to pay attention to what's going on with my mother."

Victor looked puzzled and she told him about her talk with Miss Bauman.

"Maybe she's tired and needs a break from school," he said. "I feel like that myself sometimes. It's not easy, working and going to classes, too."

"But you keep doing it because it's important to you. To her, too. I'm scared something's wrong."

Victor put his arm around her shoulder as they neared her boarding house. "Talk to her and it'll be okay, you'll see. When are we getting together? If it keeps snowing we could go sledding in Schenley Park."

"I don't have a sled," Molly said.

"Me neither, but we won't let that stop us. I'll think of something."

Molly laughed. "I bet you will. I have to go inside now, before I freeze."

"See you soon," Victor said. "I'll arrange for a dog-sled and team to race in the park."

She waved and went inside.

SIXTEEN

Hannah Klein sat at the small table, a book propped before her, but she was not reading. She stared into space, looking forlorn and weary, her skin pale, lines etched at the corners of her eyes and mouth.

When she saw Molly she attempted a smile but her eyes remained sad and dull. "You're late tonight. Busy evening with the children?"

"No more than usual, but Maria says we're going to get busier. Three new families from Rumania have started coming to the Settlement House. Their ten children don't know English, so

Maria's trying to figure out some way to include them in the learning circles. She thinks that if she finds a volunteer who speaks their language it might work . . ."

Molly saw that Hannah wasn't listening; the far-away look had returned. Her mother usually wanted to hear about school and the Settlement House. Was she sick? Would she soon begin to cough and spit blood? Molly could feel her heart thumping against her blouse. "Mama? Why don't you tell me what's wrong?"

Hannah looked down at her hands resting on the table and twisted them together. She took a deep breath, as if gathering courage for what she had to say. "Something's happened to Papa and David and I don't know what to do. It's been too long since a letter came, not like your father at all. He writes every week. I am so afraid."

She lowered her head. Although there was no sound, Molly knew she was crying. Guilt swept over her—she hadn't even noticed that her mother didn't mention letters from Swidnik. And she realized how long it had been since she mailed her own letter.

"There must be a reason—maybe he got very busy with the shop or he caught a cold and didn't feel like writing or . . ." Molly's excuses sounded feeble even to her.

"That's not so and you know it," her mother snapped, irritation replacing sadness in her voice. "Your father would never let those things stop him. Or he'd tell David to write, so I wouldn't worry. Something's wrong, something terrible has happened. I know it. Maybe, because they went to Russia for Simon's wedding, they got in trouble with the police. What if Papa's in jail someplace or so sick David doesn't want me to know? If I don't hear soon I'll go crazy."

"Did you talk to Uncle Abe about this?"

She nodded, wiping at her cheeks to stop the tears rolling down. "He says I should quit eating my heart out, that sometimes mail gets lost or is slow, or the system breaks down."

"That makes sense."

"Over four weeks? I don't think so."

"You always say Uncle Abe's smart. Why aren't you listening to him now?"

"Because he's only trying to make me feel better. He's been away from Poland for many years. What does he know about the terrible things that happen there? The arrests for no reason, the beatings, the lies they make up about innocent people?"

In her agitation, Hannah had slipped into Polish, speaking so rapidly Molly could barely understand her. "Slow down, Mama, please. You'll make yourself sick and how will that help anything? Besides, when you talk fast in Polish I don't understand what you're saying."

Hannah studied her, grim-faced. "You're such an American you forget the language now? Maybe you forget Papa and David too."

Molly could hardly believe what she heard. How could her mother say something so cruel? She wanted to scream at her, but she knew that would only make things worse. "I know you don't mean that and only say it because you're upset. You have to be patient. What Uncle Abe told you makes sense. Remember how everything in Swidnik used to break down, even pipes for the water? Why should the mail be different?"

Her mother nodded, but wasn't convinced.

"You'll see," Molly said. "In a few days you'll get three or four letters, all at once."

That didn't happen. Molly wasn't at all sure that she believed her own reassurances. She remembered what had happened to Mr. Gelman, the shoemaker; how he'd been beaten when a customer lied about him. The police had done nothing and that was what convinced her mother they had to leave.

That could have happened to her father, too. Or, maybe he was held in Russia on some faked charge, so that he and David couldn't return to Swidnik. Soon, she was nearly as fearful as her mother. Another week passed, still with no word. Her mother didn't speak of it, only grew quieter and sadder. Uncle Abe kept offering explanations in his gruff attempts to be encouraging, but Molly could tell that he, too, was worried.

Her own fears increased. She couldn't focus on school or the Settlement House. One night, her mother shook her awake. "Molly, you were yelling in your sleep. What were you dreaming about?"

"I don't remember. Probably something at school." That was a lie. In her nightmare, she was in a prison, a horrible place with cobwebs between the bars and rats scurrying into corners. Her father was in a cell, one of his eyes bruised and swollen. He was reaching out to her with bloodied fingers, calling her in Yiddish. All she understood was her name, Malke. She was screaming that she didn't understand, she couldn't help him until she knew what he was saying. Thank God her mother woke her. She was shaking. The room was cold, but her nightgown stuck to her perspiring body.

Maria commented on her unusual silences, even with the children, but Molly couldn't bring herself to explain and Maria asked no questions. Miss Cather, however, was not at all reluctant. "Molly, please wait after class today," she said as they finished a discussion of the first act of *Macbeth*. As Molly searched her mind to recall what she might've done wrong, the bell rang. She didn't think she'd forgotten any assignments and was still puzzling over it when her classmates left.

Miss Cather sat at the desk next to Molly's. "You're not in any trouble, if that's what you're looking so somber about. At least not with me."

Relieved, Molly waited.

"I've been wondering what's bothering you. It's not like you to sit quietly during class discussions. When I look in your direction, expecting a response, what I see is a blank stare, suggesting your mind is far away."

"I'm sorry. I've been trying to keep up, but you're right. I haven't been concentrating in any of my classes."

Miss Cather looked at her with a steady gaze Molly couldn't avoid. Reluctantly at first, she began to explain about the letters. Then the words poured out, along with her fears for her father and brother and worries about her mother. Molly told her teacher how her mother had been sickly in Swidnik and how her father hoped she'd get stronger in America. "I'm so afraid she'll get consumption, like a neighbor in Swidnik. Mrs. Kahn went away and . . . never came home."

Willa Cather listened without interruption, her eyes intent on Molly's face. "How long has it been since you've heard?" she asked when Molly finished.

"Over a month," Molly answered, trying to swallow past the lump in her throat.

Her teacher sighed and thought for a while before answering. "I won't attempt to pass this off lightly. That would insult your intelligence and I know enough about some countries' tyranny to believe you're right to worry. I'm so sorry you're going through this." She hesitated and thought again. "Have you spoken with Miss Bauman? She might have some ideas."

"Not yet, but I will. Maybe my mother's already told her, but she hasn't said anything to me. She doesn't go to classes, so she hasn't seen Miss Bauman lately. She comes home from the store looking sick and depressed, then just stays in our room. She tries not to, but sometimes she can't help crying in front of me."

"What about your uncle? He certainly knows how to be tough and persistent when he chooses to be."

Molly looked at Miss Cather. They both were thinking of the day he'd evicted her from the store because she asked so many annoying questions. "He acts tough, but inside he's soft-hearted, and he's as worried about Papa as we are."

She nodded. "Why don't we work on this together? There may be a way to learn more if we write to the officials at Ellis Island where immigrants first come into this country."

Molly looked doubtful. "How could that help? Besides, I don't want to write to people in power. In Poland we tried to keep the people in power from noticing us. When they did, bad things usually happened."

"You live in a democracy now, Molly. Officials' jobs are meant to help us, not harm us. They work for us in this country."

Molly's face reflected her unease. "I guess I'm still a greenhorn in America."

"Nonsense! I won't allow you to belittle the progress you've made in the time I've known you. Your English has improved so much that people unfamiliar with your background wouldn't guess you're an immigrant."

"Really?" Molly said, remembering Maria's comments but still doubtful.

"Have you ever known me to offer undeserved praise?" her teacher said.

Molly thought it wise not to say what went through her head, that Miss Cather sometimes neglected to praise students who deserved it. She shook her head.

"Indeed not," her teacher continued. "You've shown improvement in all your classes. Your other teachers assure me that you are doing well."

Surprised, Molly looked at Miss Cather, not knowing how to express her question. Had her teacher been checking up on her? Why? Was she doing something wrong?

"Stop looking so guilty! I haven't been spying. I admire you for the way you've handled problems that would discourage many adults. But I've been concerned about you because I know how awful you felt when Cleo left and how much you worry about your mother. And you're frightened for your father and brother. That's why I think we should play detective and contact Ellis Island."

Molly nodded, but having her troubles described only made her feel worse. If Miss Cather thought she could ask for help from Ellis Island, Molly would write to them tomorrow and show her letter to her teacher.

Molly looked at Miss Cather, her face brightening. "I'll start on the letter tomorrow if you'll help me," she said.

Miss Cather nodded and smiled. "I have an idea for a happy distraction. If your mother agrees, would you like to go with me this evening to see a performance of *Hamlet*? I'm to review it for the *Gazette* and I'm sure I could get an extra ticket. A traveling company from England will be performing. What do you think?"

"I'd like that. I've never seen a play."

"You must begin then, at once. This city has so many cultural attractions. Have you been to the Art Institute to see the paintings? Mr. Carnegie has started collecting beautiful pictures for Pittsburghers to enjoy."

"I only know about his library," Molly said. "Cleo and I used to borrow books there and now I go by myself. I asked Victor to come, but he said only if he could find math books. That's all he wants to know. I guess that's what people mean by a genius."

"Nonsense," Miss Cather scoffed. "Genius is another way of defining great enthusiasm. We must try to get Vittorio enthused about something besides numbers."

"Ice cream would do it," Molly answered.

"The play begins at eight, at the Newcomb Theater. It's downtown from here. Will you be able to get there?"

"I'll take a streetcar. The driver'll tell me when to get off and how to find the theater."

"Good. I'll meet you there fifteen minutes before curtain time."

Molly looked puzzled. "Curtain?"

Miss Cather smiled. "That is an odd expression, isn't it? It means the time when the play begins."

On her way home from school Molly stopped at the store to tell her mother about the invitation. Uncle Abe was there and so was Bella Bloom, but her mother wasn't. After enduring a smothering hug from Mrs. Bloom, she looked at her uncle, who said, "Your mother's gone to the Settlement House. It's not busy this afternoon, so I told her to leave early."

"She went to her class? I'm glad. She's been so worried about Papa and David lately, she hasn't been going."

"Of course she's worried, poor thing. Who wouldn't be?" Mrs. Bloom said. "My God, the way things are in Poland, who knows what can happen to innocent people? Mrs. Gold was telling me only last week about her nephew in Warsaw. His mother wrote about how the boy was picked up by the police for no reason and taken to jail where they . . ."

"Molly doesn't want to hear all the details of gossip your lady friends tell, Bella."

"It's not gossip. Mrs. Gold said that when the boy finally got out he had a broken arm, was beaten black and blue and—"

Abe gave her a sharp look and she stopped.

"I don't think your mother was going to class," Abe said. "She wanted to talk to Miss Bauman. I told her that's a good idea. I'm sure there's a logical explanation why the letters aren't getting through. Miss Bauman knows about such things and will advise her."

Molly wasn't convinced. Like her mother, she was afraid something was very wrong. "If you don't need me then, I'll go home. I have schoolwork to do and tonight I'm going to see a play."

"A play?" Uncle Abe said. "You're getting to be a regular high society lady. Are you going with Mr. Frick or Mr. Westinghouse?"

"Don't tease her, Abe, let her tell us. All these years in Pittsburgh, I've never been to a play," Mrs. Bloom interrupted.

"That's what I'm saying. A little while ago a greenhorn, now she's mixing with the rich folks. How'd this happen, Molly?"

"Sorry to disappoint you, Uncle, but I didn't get an invitation from Andrew Carnegie and he's not sending his carriage. I'm going on the streetcar to the Newcomb Theater. Miss Cather, my English teacher, invited me to see *Hamlet*."

"Mmhmm. Isn't that the high-class lady who invited you to the tea party at her fancy-shmansy house?"

Before she could answer, he turned to Mrs. Bloom. "The same nosy woman came into my store, demanding to see the cellar where I keep the chickens, so she could write a story about it. I threw her out."

Bella clapped a hand to her face. "What? From this store, you threw her out? How could you do such a thing?"

"If you'll excuse me, I've heard all this before. Goodbye, Mrs. Bloom."

The older woman nodded. "I'm always glad to see you, Molly. Have a good time tonight. Maybe you'll come visit and tell me all about the play."

As she walked home, Molly thought what an odd couple her uncle and Bella Bloom were. If only she could tell Cleo, they'd laugh about it. Cleo would have helped her now, too, when she was so scared. But Cleo was gone and Molly felt nearly as alone as when she first came to Pittsburgh.

SEVENTEEN

Molly's mother arrived shortly before dinner time. As they went downstairs to the dining room, Molly asked about her talk with Miss Bauman.

"She tried to make me feel better," Hannah said, "by telling me about the way mail is stopped by weather and politics—problems with the postal workers—or letters are sent to the wrong place." Hannah sighed as they sat down together at the long table all the boarders shared. "Some of it made sense, but not that it should take so many weeks. Sometimes the letters were late before, but never like this."

Molly couldn't think of anything comforting to say. Instead, she tried changing the subject, talking about her plans for the evening.

Her mother's face brightened. "Papa and I read that play together. It's very sad, but full of beautiful words. Have you studied it in school?"

"Not yet. You and Papa read it? When?"

"In Swidnik, long ago. Your father and his friends would sometimes trade books. He brought *Hamlet* home one night and we read it when you children were in bed."

"In English? It's so hard to understand Shakespeare's English."

Hannah nodded, remembering. Her expression softened and Molly noticed a bit of color in her cheeks. "At first we tried, but there were so many words we didn't know and they weren't in Papa's English dictionary. So he went to a bookstore and bought the play in Polish. We took turns acting out the parts, your father reading the men's lines and I the ladies'. Sometimes, when he'd jump up and shout something like 'Behold!' it was so funny I'd have to laugh. He'd say I spoiled the mood, but then he'd laugh, too."

"'Behold' must sound funny in Polish," Molly said.

"It sounds funny in English, too," Hannah replied.

Her mother's joking was so rare these days that Molly didn't complain about the cold mashed potatoes and greasy boiled beef their landlady placed before them. Back upstairs, Molly dressed in her best long woolen skirt and the yellow blouse Mrs. Payson made for her. She attached the violet pin, Cleo's gift, to her collar and thought how Cleo would want to hear about this evening. Molly couldn't tell her, but she could describe the theater and actors to her mother to give her something nice to think about. She'd hope, too, that her father would be able to read a letter about the play he and Mama acted out in Polish while their children slept. She would write to him and describe it . . . and pray that he received it.

By the time she climbed the streetcar steps, she was feeling cheerier. There were few riders; Molly absent-mindedly looked out the window. What she saw wasn't rows of houses and stores, but a cozy kitchen with a bench before the wood fire and father and daughter, heads bent together over a book.

Papa had been so patient when she stumbled over the English words, making up jokes about the funny sounds. In his shop, he let her play with the colored threads and scraps of cloth left over from trousers and jackets. Once, he'd made her a doll of patches and ribbons that she kept beside her every night. It must still be in her room in Swidnik. Sometimes she hid behind the racks where he hung the clothing and he pretended he couldn't find her. Now he was hidden—what if she could never find him? She mustn't cry—what would the driver and the woman sitting across from her think? And she would upset Miss Cather, who wanted her to be happy at the theater tonight.

After she got off and followed the driver's directions, Molly found the theater and realized she was early. That was all right; she could study her surroundings and watch the people arriving for the performance. She'd never seen the Newcomb Theater; it was grander than any building she'd encountered and only a few years old, Miss Cather had said. Creamy and bright among dark stone neighbors, its five stories rose to a graceful dome in the center of the roof. Carriages stopped at the canopied entrance. Molly watched as women in long satin dresses and plush furs swept through the wide doors. Men wearing black suits and stiff-collared white shirts accompanied them.

"Are you enjoying the spectacle of the fluffy-ruffles people?" said a voice behind her. Molly turned to see Miss Cather grinning at her. Her teacher looked quite special herself in an ankle-length dress of turquoise topped by a brown velvet jacket. A tortoise comb, set with small amber stones, was tucked into her upswept hair.

"People are dressed as if they're going to a fancy party."

"They are," Miss Cather said as they walked into the large lobby, noisy with conversation and shouted greetings. "Going to the theater is a social event for most of them. They come not so much to see the play as each other and to be seen in their finery. If you listen you'll hear gossip about dinner parties or, among the men, profitable business schemes. Soon, a chime will sound and everyone will leave the lobby and go inside to the theater. People will keep talking until the lights dim. Then comes the best moment of all. The room goes dark and silent, the curtain rises, and we're in Denmark, on the parapets of the royal castle."

She looked at Molly, who listened as she stole glances at the people around her. "Our seats are on the first balcony, so we'd better go inside and start climbing."

"The first balcony?" Molly said as they joined the ascending crowd.

"There's a second balcony, much higher than where we're sitting. It's where the least expensive seats are, affordable for theater lovers who aren't interested in the social display. Students buy tickets in that section and some immigrant families will save extra pennies until they have enough for tickets."

"That's probably what my parents would do," Molly said and told Miss Cather her mother's story of reading the play.

"It's hard to imagine Shakespeare's words in Polish—or Chinese, for that matter," Miss Cather said, smiling. "I suspect that wily old playwright would be amused and delighted at the idea."

An usher approached them as they stood in the balcony's main aisle and led them to their seats. Molly gazed around the huge hall filling with people, then down at the stage, hidden behind a heavy red velvet curtain. She looked at the program the usher gave her, listing the actors and describing the settings for each scene of the play.

"What do you think, Molly?" her teacher asked, looking up from a notebook where she'd been jotting some lines.

"It's so beautiful! It must be at least as grand as the place in London where Shakespeare directed his plays."

"Much more elaborate," Miss Cather responded. "The Globe Theater was far simpler, with only the most basic props and costumes. Audiences had to use their imaginations much more than we will tonight to be transported to the world of Prince Hamlet. In this performance you'll see costumes, sets, and lighting that the

Elizabethans never dreamed of. Their plays had to be performed in daylight, remember, with torches to remind them when it was supposed to be night."

Molly nodded, continuing to inspect her surroundings.

"And the people on the first floor," Miss Cather continued, "the ones in the fancy furs you were admiring, could well be sitting on the stage for a performance in Shakespeare's time. Those theater lovers in the balcony above us would be the groundlings, standing in the pit around the stage, throwing rotten fruit if they didn't like the show."

Molly turned in her seat, craning her neck to look up at the second balcony. "They look much too polite to do that," she said.

"Lucky for us, because we'd be directly in the path of mushy flying objects."

Molly grinned, imagining Miss Cather's carefully arranged hairstyle topped with a dripping tomato.

The lights dimmed and her teacher whispered, "The play's about to start. Pay no attention to my scribbling. The notes are reminders of what I intend to say in my review for the paper, but don't let my writing distract you."

She needn't have been concerned. From the moment the curtain rose to reveal the gloomy towers of the royal castle, guards pacing and muttering their fears of a ghost, Molly was entranced. Her attention never wavered and when the curtain descended for the first intermission she was sorry, eager for the play to begin again.

Like the others around them, she and Miss Cather stood, stretched, and commented on the performance. "With so much happening onstage, how can you write about the play in a short article?" Molly said.

"It isn't easy," Miss Cather answered, closing her notebook and turning to Molly. "Sometimes I think it's presumptuous to try to condense the essence of a great work like *Hamlet* into a few column lengths of newsprint. I try to remember the purpose of my review: helping people decide if they want to spend their hard-earned money to see this particular production. Reminding myself of that, I can describe the quality of the performance and whether this company does credit to the play. What do you think I should tell my readers?"

"To come see it! Everything about it's perfect. The actors make the words sound like music."

"Give Shakespeare some credit for that," her teacher said.

"Yes, but when we read a play for homework and the words only sound in our heads, it's not the same. The actors make Hamlet, Ophelia, and the others real people."

"That's good critical judgment. I may quote you in my review," Miss Cather said.

"Tell them how beautiful the theater is, too, and about the audience in their fancy clothes."

"The fluffy ruffles? The actors would be happier with your praise than all the polite applause from the overdressed ladies."

"Does that mean Shakespeare's actors liked the groundlings best?"

Miss Cather smiled. "I hadn't thought about that but I suspect they appreciated honest critics who either cheered or jeered— both loudly."

"But the fluffy-ruffles would never throw rotten fruit," Molly added. "They wouldn't want it to drip on their furs."

Miss Cather's guffaw caused the people in the row in front of them to turn and glare. "I may use that in an article, too, but one I'll write for the people back in Nebraska, not Pittsburgh. We wouldn't want to offend the local patrons of the arts."

The lights dimmed again and Molly, sighing with pleasure, sat back to watch the rest of the play. Transported into Hamlet's world, for a few hours she forgot about her own. When the drama ended she rose and joined in the applause, clapping until her palms stung.

"I didn't want it to end, even though the last act was so sad. Seeing a play is like living in someone else's world."

"If it's a good play and well performed," her teacher said. "I've seen some where the acting was so dreadful that lines meant to be serious brought hoots of laughter from the audience."

"Did you have to write reviews of them?"

"Sometimes. I have to be honest, even if it means hurting careers. When that happens I tell myself that people so bad at their craft shouldn't be working in the theater. Artists should be dedicated and single-minded in honoring and pursuing their talents if they hope to enhance the lives of others."

"What does 'enhance' mean?" Molly said.

When Miss Cather explained Molly asked, "Do you feel that way about writing?"

"If I didn't I wouldn't even try. Real artists give up too much of normal life, so it has to be worth the effort."

"I wish Cleo could have seen the play," Molly said.

"You must still miss her a lot."

Molly nodded. "Cleo made me feel as if I belong here. Sometimes, without her, it's like when I first came and was so lonely and embarrassed at being different."

"If it helps," Miss Cather said, "I feel that way sometimes, too. It's related to what I was saying about artists, Molly. But we'll both muddle through just fine."

EIGHTEEN

Molly thought about Miss Cather's words as the trolley sped through dark streets, back to the Hill. She hadn't considered the sacrifices made by writers and other artists—only their fame and the praise they received. Molly felt lucky about her own plans: she'd be helping people as a social worker, but still enjoying other parts of life. Maybe Miss Cather was willing to give up raising a family; not Molly. Her mother cherished that role and she wanted it for herself, too.

Thinking about her mother jarred Molly out of Shakespeare's world and back into her own, a sad and frightening place now. She had to find some way to help her mother. Molly was sure Miss Bauman was doing what she could, but there must be something more her own daughter could do. Despite Miss Cather's optimism, she didn't expect much help from Ellis Island. Maybe she could write to one of her former friends in Swidnik. But what could she say? "My father is missing. Can you help to find him?" That was crazy. She'd have to find another way.

She climbed the stairs slowly, trying to postpone the inevitable gloomy encounter with her mother. Approaching the room they shared, Molly heard voices. It was late for visitors and one of the voices was Uncle Abe's. Something had happened! She felt sick and weak in the knees. What if her mother had collapsed, with the consumption Molly feared? Someone found her and had gone for Uncle Abe because Molly was out enjoying herself while her mother lay coughing and bleeding! She shivered and pushed open the door.

There were three people in the room with Mama, who was sitting on the bed, weeping. Beside her was a thin, bearded man, his lined face dominated by large brown eyes concentrating on her mother. His arm was around her shoulders and she was leaning against him.

A younger man, knapsack on the floor near him, stood next to Uncle Abe, who was grinning around the big cigar clamped in his mouth.

As Molly stared, the man beside her mother looked at her, uncomprehending. Then, eyes filling with tears, he rose, put his hands on her shoulders, studied her face, and spoke in the soft voice she recognized as her father's.

"Molly, my American daughter! You've grown into such a beautiful young woman, I couldn't find the little girl who left me."

He held her in his arms and Molly's fears dissolved into a wordless joy.

"That's not Molly, Papa. She's an American actress pretending to be part of our family. But, maybe not. My little sister always liked to play teasing games."

Molly turned to look at the tall, handsome stranger standing beside Uncle Abe. Eyes full of merriment, he'd been unrecognizable until he smiled. It was the mischievous grin she remembered. "David!" she screamed and rushed to hug him. Then she looked around at the others and said, "How did all this happen? When did you get here?"

Everyone erupted into speech until Uncle Abe shouted, "Quiet! Who can make any sense of all this jabbering? Everybody sit down, take a deep breath, and talk one at a time." Then he commandeered one of the two chairs in the room, puffed on his cigar, and waited.

Molly insisted that David take the remaining chair and plopped to the floor beside him, holding his hand. The bulky knapsack and small suitcase took up most of the remaining space.

"We were so worried," Molly said. "Did the Polish police forbid you to write to us? That would never happen in America."

Her father smiled and said, "I see, Hannah, there's nothing left of old country meekness in our daughter."

"Damn right. And you should be glad," Abe said, chewing on the cigar that was now reduced to a stub.

"Uncle, please do not swear in front of the children," their father said and Molly and David exchanged amused glances. "And do you always smoke such terrible-smelling cigars?"

Molly tried not to laugh. Now that Papa was here there was finally someone to stand up to her uncle.

Abe grinned. "Not here a day and already my nephew's giving orders. That's good, good for your future." He noticed the questioning looks from the others and added, mysteriously, "Later. Now, tell us how you two managed to show up at my place looking for your family."

Hannah nestled against her husband as he, despite the frequent interruptions, told their story. Permission to leave Swidnik had come suddenly one afternoon, with instructions to depart immediately. They didn't even have time to sell their few possessions. They left neighbors in charge of the tailor shop until new tenants came. They packed clothing, food, some small things—photographs, the candlesticks that had belonged to Nathan's mother, books, and a tablecloth Hannah embroidered—into one suitcase and a knapsack, and left Swidnik. The furniture remaining behind would be for the family who took over the tailor shop and living quarters.

There was no time to write as they raced to make the trains and then the ship that would bring them to America.

"I liked sailing on the ocean, but the sea was rough. Papa got sick," David said.

"Only a weak stomach and no appetite," Nathan reassured his wife when Hannah looked anxiously at her husband. "David ate enough for both of us and went out on the deck to meet other young people and to watch the storm clouds."

"I liked the fresh air, the wind and salt smell of the sea. Inside—phew! Stale air, sick people. Especially way down near the bottom of the ship where we slept."

Molly was surprised at how well her brother spoke English and said so.

"You think you're the only one to study? I do not plan to be a greenhorn with a baby sister making fun of me."

"I wouldn't do that—much," Molly said. "Besides, you'll soon find some silly girl and make eyes at her the way Simon used to do in Swidnik. And she'll help you to understand words you don't know."

"Or teach him some new ones," Uncle Abe added with a wink.

Their mother frowned at him.

"When we got off the ship," Nathan Klein continued, "we were in New York, but not New York. We had to be on some island . . ."

"Ellis Island," Molly said. "People at the Settlement House talk about it, how the doctors examine you and if you have any sickness, even a little eye infection, you're quarantined and they don't let you . . ."

"Molly, Papa was speaking. You should let him tell what happened," Mama said.

"It's fine," Papa said, smiling. "I'm proud my daughter knows so much. We did have to stay on that island for all the tests and questions and papers to fill out. Lucky for David and me we knew a little English. Many of the others, poor things, didn't understand what was happening. The translators were too busy to take time to answer questions."

"Papa helped with the Polish and some Russian he understood," David added.

They listened as Papa and David continued their story. After they were finally cleared at Ellis Island, they had to find their way from New York to Pittsburgh.

"We came on the train," David said. "The countryside looked nice. All those hills and trees, beautiful with the snow on them. As we got close to Pittsburgh we saw the factories . . ."

"Steel mills," Uncle Abe interrupted.

"Ssh, let him talk," Mama said, making Molly smile. Now that Papa was beside her she was brave enough to criticize Uncle Abe, too.

"What a sight! Flames jumping from tall chimneys. Burning sparks flying from carts rolling on rows of tracks. Iron blocks that glowed in the dark like red eyes. And so loud! I never saw such things before."

"You'll get used to it," Molly said. "It goes on all the time here. You'll even get used to the smoke and the soot that flies through the air and lands on window sills."

"And puts food on the table for most of the people around here," Abe added.

"Food!" Mama said, looking distressed. "We've been talking and I didn't think about it. You must be so hungry."

"We're fine, Hannah," her husband said. "We had apples, bread, some cheese on the train. I'm so happy we're all together I can't think of anything else."

"I have something to say that will make you happier," Abe said. "Nathan, when you found my place tonight, did you look at my store?"

"I don't understand."

"The building, the shop, anything?"

"I saw that you live above the poultry store. But I knew that already from Hannah's letters," he said.

"What you don't know is that it's a good business, but I'm getting old and I want some time to take it easy, enjoy myself. In this country they call it retiring. So, I'm going to retire." Then he looked shy, embarrassed. "I'm even going to get married again."

The others all started to speak at once, congratulating him in a babble of languages.

"Wait, wait, enough time for that later. Besides, you should say these things to Bella. Women like to hear that sticky stuff. I'm not through with my news."

He looked at them again. "When I decided all this, I had a plan for you, but I didn't want to say anything because who knew when you could get out of Poland. After Hannah didn't get letters for such a long time I thought maybe you were on the way. But, again, I couldn't know for sure and, God forbid, something terrible might've happened to you. So I didn't say anything to Hannah. Time kept passing, Bella wanted only to talk about getting married, and I couldn't settle anything about the store. Now, I can. I'm giving it to you, Nathan."

When his nephew started to speak, Abe waved a hand for silence. "You don't need to say a thing. I have no children to take over; you're the closest to a son I'll ever have. If you want, later, when you have everything under control, you can pay me something from the profits."

"I'll be moving into Bella's house, so you and your family can live in the apartment over the store. It's no castle, but with three rooms, the kitchen, and a nice couch in the front room for David, you'll have enough space until you move to a house of your own. Molly can keep going to Central High and David, until he figures out what he wants to do besides being a millionaire, can help in the store and learn the business. So, what do you think?"

Hannah was crying again and alternately hugging her husband and his uncle. Nathan was shaking his hand and thanking him in three languages.

During a momentary lull, Molly said, "This is great, but can you talk some more in the morning? It's late, I have to go to school tomorrow and, right now, we need to figure out what part of the floor each of us will sleep on."

Uncle Abe shook his head. "That's Molly, always the organizer. She's getting as bossy as that teacher of hers. The uppity one who took her to see a play tonight."

David looked at his sister, a question beginning to form.

"Don't worry, she'll tell you all about it, but not tonight," Abe said. "For now, you and your Papa will come back to my place where there's more room and you can have a bath and a good sleep. When you're rested we'll make plans for you all to move in. Tomorrow, I'll tell Bella she'll finally have her way and get to be a bride."

Molly tried to imagine Mrs. Bloom in a long white dress that was too tight at the seams, her double chins jiggling under a veil. She couldn't help giggling. Her mother, looking at her, must have guessed her thoughts. Laughter was in her eyes now and deep in her throat. That was the sound that echoed in Molly's ears later, when the others were gone, and her mother had finally fallen asleep.

Tomorrow, Molly thought, she'd have a lot to tell Miss Cather.

HISTORICAL NOTE

The city inhabited by Molly and her friends was a very different place than the one today's readers would encounter. Molly's neighborhood was originally known as Coal Hill, Pittsburgh's eastern boundary until the late 1840s. Its first residents were wealthy city leaders who enjoyed the gently rolling hills and green countryside surrounding them.

After the Civil War, Pittsburgh's population grew rapidly— nearly a half-million people lived there. Willa Cather, in the late nineteenth century, described it as "pulsing with the incandescence of human energy."

Industrial development expanded, creating a fierce demand for factory products. The manufacture of iron and steel, glass and aluminum required enormous amounts of smoke-producing coal. In 1888, the Homestead Works of United States Steel began open-hearth production and in Braddock the Edgar Thomson Works started continuous operation. The city gained a dubious reputation as a place of grime, smoke, and unremitting soot and smog.

Streetcars were introduced in 1888, providing access to cleaner places away from the industrial heart of the city. Those who could afford to often followed the trolley lines to life in cleaner neighborhoods and the Hill District became the densely crowded habitat of the poor.

Between 1870 and 1890 masses of immigrants arrived in Pittsburgh: Jews fleeing the oppression of eastern European ghettos; Italians and Greeks, Poles and Syrians hoping for better lives in America. African-Americans streamed into the city from the South, seeking job opportunities. Everyone crowded together in ramshackle tenements that were often poorly built and unsanitary.

Pittsburgh was home not only to struggling and overworked new Americans, but also to a wealthy community of industrialists and entrepreneurs. Eager to improve their community and its reputation, they supported art, music, theaters, and an impressive array of charities and public services. Families whose names are familiar to many Americans—Mellon, Westinghouse, Frick, Carnegie—made their homes and their fortunes in the city. They enriched its cultural life with a great museum, elegant concert halls and theaters, a fine symphony orchestra, and an unparalleled system of public libraries that were—and are—free and available to every citizen.

Although the residents of Pittsburgh's Hill District had to struggle with poverty and the daily onslaught of grime and smoke, they, like their fictional representatives, were energetic and determined people whose courage and strength improved the lives of their families and their descendants.

AUTHOR

Anne Gussin Faigen's first young adult novel, *Finding Her Way*, was published in 1997. A native Pittsburgher with a B.A. in creative writing from the University of Pittsburgh and a graduate degree in literature, she has taught college literature and writing classes and had a long career as a teacher of honors and advanced placement English to high school students.

A book reviewer and freelance journalist, Anne Faigen is also a volunteer reader of novels at RIS, the Pittsburgh radio station for the blind and visually handicapped. The author is married, the mother of grown children, and has five grandchildren.

TEACHER'S STUDY GUIDE AVAILABLE FOR

NEW WORLD WAITING

Teacher Marcy Canterna has developed a practical and grade appropriate study guide for teachers to accompany Anne Faigen's factually-based novel for young readers. The book's vocabulary makes it appropriate for older elementary grades, while the factual material included will make it interesting to more advanced students. The study guide includes exercises for readers at these different levels. Available from the publisher.

For details, you can contact us by telephone at:

  412-362-2294.

Or Email us at:

  Sales@TheLocalHistoryCompany.com

Or visit our website:

  www.TheLocalHistoryCompany.com

Or write us at:

  Sales
  The Local History Company
  112 North Woodland Road
  Pittsburgh, PA 15232-2849

ORDER ADDITIONAL COPIES OF

ANNE G. FAIGEN'S

NEW WORLD WAITING
(ISBN 0-9744715-5-0)

and Marcy Canterna's
Teacher's Study Guide

from THE LOCAL HISTORY COMPANY
Publishers of History and Heritage
www.TheLocalHistoryCompany.com
Sales@TheLocalHistoryCompany.com

ORDER FORM—PLEASE PRINT CLEARLY

NAME _____

COMPANY (if applicable) _____

ADDRESS _____

CITY _____ STATE _____ ZIP _____

PHONE _____ We require your phone number so we can contact you in case there is a problem with your order. Your privacy is important to us: We do not sell or trade your personal information with others.

Please allow 2-4 weeks for delivery. Prices subject to change without notice. All book sales are final. US shipments only (contact us for information on international orders). Payable by check, money order, or Visa/MasterCard in US funds.

PLEASE SEND _____ copies of New World Waiting at $17.95 each ..Subtotal: $_____

PLEASE SEND _____ copies of Teacher's Study Guide at $7.95 each ..Subtotal: $_____

ITEM Subtotal: $_____

PA Sales Tax: PA residents (outside Allegheny County) add 6% of Item Subtotal, or if resident of Allegheny County, PA add 7% of Item Subtotal $_____

Add $5 packaging/shipping for the first item and $1 each additional item $_____

TOTAL AMOUNT DUE: $_____

PAYMENT BY CHECK/MONEY ORDER:
_____ Enclosed is my check/money order for the total amount due made payable to:
The Local History Company

PAYMENT BY VISA OR MasterCard Credit Card:
Bill my _____ Visa _____ MasterCard Account # _____
(Address above must be the same as on file with your credit card company)

Expires _____ Name as it appears on your card _____

Signature _____

Mail or Fax your order to: The Local History Company
(FAX 412-362-8192) 112 NORTH Woodland Road
Pittsburgh, PA 15232-2849
Or—Call 412-362-2294 with your order.